"Reigna." He called with a quiet strength that let her know he was in control of this conversation. **"I am Jasiri Issa Nguvu of the royal house of Adébísí, son of King Omari Jasiri Sahel of the royal house of Adébísí, crown prince and heir apparent to the throne of Nyeusi."**

Her jaw dropped as her eyes searched for any hint that he was joking. Unfortunately, the straight set of his jaw and his level gaze didn't say, "Girl, you know I'm just playing with you." Nope, that was a "No lies detected" face staring back at her.

"You're...you're a...prince?"

"Not a prince, *the* prince. As the heir to the throne, I stand above all other princes in the royal line."

She peeled her hand away from the armrest and pointed to herself. "And that makes me...?"

He continued smoothly as if they were having a normal everyday conversation and not one that was literally life-changing. "As my wife, you are now Princess Reigna of the royal house of Adébísí, consort to the heir and future queen of Nyeusi."

A dazzling new duet for Harlequin Presents
from author LaQuette.

Crowning a Devereaux

*By royal decree, the Devereaux sisters will be
crowned!*

Identical twins and business partners Reigna and
Regina Devereaux were born to lead—they just
didn't realize that included a kingdom.

When ex-lover Jasiri charges back into Reigna's life
with an arranged-marriage offer, she never imagined
it would mean becoming his crown princess! But
he's offering to return to her the inheritance that he
was wrongfully given... So Reigna says "I do"...only to
find that even royal duty cannot keep their attraction
from roaring back to life!

Royal Bride Demand

Look out for Regina's story, coming soon!

ROYAL BRIDE DEMAND

LaQUETTE

PRESENTS

**Harlequin®
PRESENTS™**

ISBN-13: 978-1-335-63178-7

Royal Bride Demand

Recycling programs for this product may not exist in your area.

 Harlequin Enterprises ULC
22 Adelaide St. West, 41st Floor
Toronto, Ontario M5H 4E3, Canada
www.Harlequin.com

Printed in U.S.A.

A 2021 Vivian Award finalist and DEIA activist in the romance industry, **LaQuette** writes sexy, stylish and sensational romance. She crafts dramatic, emotionally epic tales that are deeply pigmented by reality's paintbrush.

This Brooklyn native writes unapologetically bold, character-driven stories. Her novels feature diverse ensemble casts that are confident in their right to appear on the page.

Contact: dot.cards/laquette

Books by LaQuette

This is LaQuette's debut book for
Harlequin Presents—we hope that you enjoy it!

Harlequin Desire

Devereaux, Inc

A Very Intimate Takeover
Backstage Benefits
One Night Expectations
Secret Heir for Christmas

Visit the Author Profile page
at Harlequin.com for more titles.

To sixteen-year-old LaQuette, who never thought she'd see herself, a curvy Black Brooklyn diva, in the pages of a Harlequin Presents royal romance, and to curvy Black divas, all divas, across the globe. Reigna and Jasiri's story proves that epic love and beauty come in all shapes, sizes, colors, cultures and geographical locations.

CHAPTER ONE

"I DON'T CARE who he's meeting with or how many guards you have at this consulate. I want to see him right now!"

Prince Jasiri smiled as the familiar sharp tones of an angry woman pierced the heavy walls of the consulate. Reigna Devereaux was finally here, a full day earlier than he'd expected too.

From the moment Sherard informed him of Ace's death yesterday, he'd known Reigna would end up on his doorstep. Ace Devereaux was Reigna's beloved great-uncle who had swooped in when things were at their worst with her parents and protected Reigna and her identical twin sister, Regina. He'd doted on them, given them the parental support and love their parents failed to provide, and according to Reigna, he was the only reason the twin girls grew up with any joy in their childhood. As a result, Reigna and her sister were devoted to Ace.

Considering how much the man meant to her, Jasiri wagered it would take her a few days to process this enormous loss. Despite her grief, however, she was apparently ready to wage war if her loud bellow in the hall was any indication.

"I guess the show begins now."

He readjusted his big body in the large office chair before pressing the button on the intercom on his desk.

"Bring her to my office" was all he said before ending the connection. When you were a man with as much power as he, there was no need to explain yourself. Those in your service simply did what you said without question. Something the woman currently yelling at his staff had never learned to do.

He took a calming breath as he anticipated how this impromptu meeting would unfold. Reigna might not have learned how to listen in the past. But now that he had something she wanted, thanks to Ace Devereaux, he was certain she'd submit the same way everyone else around Jasiri did: completely and without question.

The carpeted flooring couldn't stop the echo of her heavy footfalls as she walked toward his office. Knowing she was angry, knowing why she was angry made his heart thump hard against his chest with the sweet taste of revenge on the tip of his tongue.

Two years ago, it had been him who was marching to her office, mad as hell and seeking answers. Today…well, today, the spoiled society princess Reigna Devereaux would finally get what was coming to her, and he couldn't wait. He hadn't planned it this way. He'd not spent the last two years planning Reigna's destruction. Holding on to a grudge this long wasn't his usual way. But his father's life was hanging in the balance, and if that meant inconveniencing Reigna, even for a little bit, he would do what he had to do to keep his father healthy and alive. He'd do whatever he must to keep his country safe from the likes of Pili.

His adjutant, Sherard, was only able to get the door open halfway before Reigna pushed her way through, heading directly for his desk. Sherard followed her inside of the room and waited for Jasiri to give a soft nod before he exited, leaving the two of them alone for the first time in two years.

"You arrogant prick. You did this."

Her sharp words drew his gaze and instantly his sight was filled with her lovely form. Reigna was a beautiful plus-size woman, with plentiful curves, and deep brown skin. Curves and skin he'd spent hours admiring with his eyes, his hands, and his body. After two years of separation, he'd hoped the only thing the sight of her physical attributes did was remind him that she was off-limits, tainted by the memory of their failed past. Unfortunately, the straining muscles of his body and his racing heart made it apparent her effect on him wasn't as benign as he'd hoped.

"I've done a lot of things, Reigna. Many that would get me labeled much worse things than an *arrogant prick*. So you'll need to be a bit more specific if you want me to understand what you're referring to."

Her jaw tightened as she glared at him, and the spectacle of her standing in his office, thrumming with anger, made his lips bend into a smile. The first rule of conquering an enemy was to let them see just how little they meant to you. And after turning down his marriage proposal and rejecting him, Reigna meant less than nothing to him. His body might disagree, but his head knew the truth. She was simply a means to an end.

"You got Uncle Ace to leave you half of the house that was supposed to be mine alone."

"Supposed to be?" he quipped. "If that were the case, wouldn't it have worked out that way?"

"Listen, I don't know what you did to get Ace to do this, but I am going to fight to overturn it." She huffed, pointing her finger at him as she geared up for what he assumed would be more vitriol. "I knew you were a piece of work, but I never thought you'd stoop so low as to steal my childhood home just to get back at me for the great sin of turning your proposal down. It's been two years already, Jasiri. Get the hell over it."

"It *has* been two years," he countered, his speech slow but intentional. "And trust me, I *am* well over *it* and *you*. But I haven't forgotten a thing about your betrayal, Reigna. Our history notwithstanding, I didn't do anything to make Ace give me half ownership of that house. He called me into his office two years ago and gave it to me. He said I would need it one day, and it appears he was right, because here we are."

He could see the question folding into her pinched brow before she uttered it. "Then, why would Ace do this?"

He shrugged, relaxing even more as her anger bled into bewilderment. "I wouldn't know."

She narrowed her gaze as she leaned over his desk, placing her hands flat on its surface. "Then, if you didn't ask Ace for the house, does that mean you'd be willing to sell me your half of the ownership?"

There it was, the selfish, spoiled brat she'd

always been, climbing up to see how she could make a situation beneficial for herself first and foremost.

"Reigna," he said with amusement in his tone as he tilted his head to the side. "I didn't ask Ace for this gift, but you should know I have no intention of parting with it."

He could see the tightness in her features return as her ire burned a deep red beneath her skin. "Why the hell not? The place holds no significance to you. It's my childhood home, the place I…"

"Felt the most love. The place where your life was the most perfect after your parents' divorce? I know."

She'd said those exact words to him time and time again over their two-year courtship. He'd admired her emotional attachment to the place then. Now he was counting on that very same attachment to give him the power over her he needed to wield if he was going to save his father.

"You're doing this just to hurt me." Her words were spoken on a soft breath, but they were heavy and impactful all the same.

In her eyes, he could see the cloud of hurt mixed with grief and part of him, a tiny sliver, wanted to pull her in his arms and tell her it would be all right. Damn this woman and the hold she'd always had over him. He shook his head, refusing to give in. She might have fooled him before, but now he knew better. Reigna didn't want him. And no matter how good her body made his feel, he could not let those memories make him vulnerable to her. If he was to protect his father and his nation, he had to do what was necessary.

"Reigna, I'd have to care about you to be concerned with hurting you." He could see the involuntary flinch she tried hard to hide. Good. He needed her to know exactly where they stood with one another if his plan was going to work. "Spite is the last thing on my mind." She might not believe him, but it was the truth. He wasn't doing this just to anger her. That was a bonus. He was doing this because he had to, because all would be lost if he didn't.

"Then, why do you want it?"

He stood up from his chair, walking around it until he stood close enough to her that he could smell the spicy fragrance she was wearing floating up from her skin.

"You, Reigna. I need you. And owning half of this house gets me exactly that."

"What the hell could you possibly want from me?"

"That's simple," he smiled. "I need you to marry me."

* * *

"What the hell?"

That was all she could manage after Jasiri's unexpected declaration. Two years ago, he'd been spitting mad when he'd stormed from her office after she'd told him she wasn't ready to be a wife.

"Jasiri, you made it very clear two years ago that you didn't want me if I didn't accept your proposal. Why would you want me now?"

He sat on the front of his desk, stretching his long legs out as he casually crossed one ankle over the other. Her breath caught as she marveled at the sexy picture he made. In or out of clothes, Jasiri had the most tempting body she'd ever known. A fact that hadn't changed in the last two years since they'd broken up.

She could feel the blood rushing through her as memories of how he once used that strong, broad body of his to keep her writhing in pleasure. And even though she was livid that he'd stolen her family home from her, she couldn't shake the need being this near to him caused.

"I didn't say I wanted you, Reigna." His mouth hitched in a sinister smile. "I said I needed you. There is a difference, and you'd do well to appreciate that."

She could tell from the cold glare in his eyes that his pointing out that distinction was meant to cut her, and it certainly did. Who wouldn't be offended if the man they'd once loved with all their heart plainly laid out that he couldn't give a damn about them?

But Reigna was a Devereaux, and she'd be damned if she let this pompous man with his proper diction and his oversize ego see she was the slightest bit bothered by his lack of feeling for her or the time they'd shared together.

"Fine, then," she huffed, trying her best to present a bored affect. "Why do you *need* me to marry you?"

The answer to her question really didn't matter. It was just curiosity that was driving her to ask it. No matter what he said, once again, the answer would be no. Before, it was because she was building Gemini Queens cosmetics with Regina. Now, it was because he was an arrogant, entitled jerk who, from the confidence swimming in his dark eyes, thought he had her where he wanted her.

"My father is ill, Reigna."

He folded his arms, his body tensing before her as a dark shadow fell over his dark brown skin. She could almost feel the tension emanating from his being. Instantly, she could feel a chink in the brick wall she'd erected from the moment she'd entered the consulate.

Without realizing it, she stepped closer to

him, laying a hand on his. Purely running on instinct, she sat next to him and said, "I'm so sorry to hear that, Jasiri. The few times I video-called with your parents, they were both always so kind and gracious to me."

"Thank you for that." He whispered softly. "He always did and still does hold you in the highest esteem."

Her fingers wrapped tighter around his and warmth flowed through her. She wasn't sure why it mattered that his father still thought of her kindly, but it did.

"While I regret to hear of his poor health, that still doesn't explain what you need from me."

His jaw flexed, the muscle there jerking as he prepared to continue. "The office he holds back home has put a great deal of pressure and stress on his health. His doctors say if he doesn't re-linquish his duties, he could die. I won't let that happen, so I'm stepping into the role. Unfortu-nately, there's an archaic law on the books that forbids me from succeeding my father unless I'm married. Since this is a pressing matter and I don't have time to find a wife in the usual manner, I need you to fulfill the role."

Amusement bubbled up in her chest, spill-ing through her lips in a loud laugh until she nearly doubled over.

"I'm glad you find my father's failing health amusing."

His words cut her laughter short, and she leaned closer to him, closer than good sense warranted. Now she could smell that perfect mix of cool, sultry sweetness and him that she'd always loved to inhale whenever he'd held her.

"You know damn well I'm not laughing about your father's health."

Her rising anger should've pushed back the flashes of their past where her sense memory of that smell was taking her. Instantly she remembered long nights of their bodies pressing together until they were blissfully exhausted and damp with sweat. She tried to brace herself against them, but moments of them enveloped in each other's arms attacked her senses, forcing her to shake her head.

She didn't need to remember that. That was past, they were two different people, and currently he was holding her family home hostage. Forgetting that would put her at a disadvantage in these weird negotiations they were broaching.

She'd come here to get her family home back. Taking a trip down memory lane wasn't part of that.

"Since we both know this can't possibly be a real proposition, how about we begin the real negotiations. I'm willing to buy you out with a generous offer that's well above market value. Name your price, and I'll cut you a check."

"This is not a joke, Reigna."

She inhaled deeply, trying hard to gather her thoughts and keep her focus. Being around Jasiri had always mesmerized her. But falling into that old habit now would cost her too much.

"Why me, Jasiri? We both know as a fancy ambassador, there have got to be a bunch of women back home who would jump at the chance to marry you."

"There are," he agreed. "But my father doesn't want me to marry just to take on his duties. He's a romantic and wants me to marry for love. You're the only woman I've been romantically involved with that my father has more than passing knowledge of." He folded his arms, casting his soft gaze down to her, making her want to pull him into her arms. "If I marry you, he won't be stressed, and he'll let me take over his duties without further worry. My only goal is to protect my father, Reigna. Can you understand that?"

She definitely could. Especially after losing Ace, she understood more than most what happened when you lost someone you loved. But this? This couldn't be the answer.

"Jasiri, my heart goes out to your father. You're mistaken if you think this is the solution, though. Come on, let's get down to the real negotiations because we both know me marrying you isn't going to happen."

He tilted his head, considering her for a moment before he stood, stepping in front of her, filling up her senses as his hard gaze bore down on her.

"You misunderstand the situation, Reigna." He brought his large hand to her face, gently cupping her cheek. The feel of his skin against hers made need explode inside her. Her pulse ticked up and her breath lodged in her throat of anticipation of what his next move would be.

When they were together, him cupping her cheek was always followed by his full lips pressing against hers. She should be angered by that idea; she should be pushing him away. But as his eyes bore down into hers, her body decided—without her permission—that it would stay in this exact spot waiting for Jasiri to put her out of her misery and finally kiss her.

He was so close to her, all she had to do was lean in and their lips would touch. But she was frozen, too afraid to press forward and too hurt to walk away.

"There are no negotiations." His voice was strong but quiet, lulling her into an almost trancelike state. "These are my terms. If you want full ownership of that house, you'll have to marry me and live in my country as my devoted wife for two years. Refuse, and I will keep Ace Devereaux's very generous gift, and you'll just have to deal with me..."

He leaned down, the heat of his nearness scorching her, as the deep rumble of his voice caressed the shell of her ear.

"Forever."

She was slightly dizzy, and her pulse was elevated, reactions that could come from anger and desire. But the problem was she couldn't tell which was causing her to feel this way. Anger she could deal with. But desire...that was a totally different matter altogether and so very dangerous to her well-being. Because wanting Jasiri Adebesi was a weakness she couldn't afford to succumb to if she was going to get her family's home back.

"So what's your answer, Reigna? Do you accept my terms?"

She stepped back, needing to get her bearings because there was no way she could think clearly with him sucking up all the oxygen in her personal space.

Once she'd put a safe amount of distance between them, she straightened her shoulders and stiffened her spine. Jasiri might be a powerful ambassador for his country, but she was determined that he would have no power over her.

He raised a brow, showing her he was still waiting for her answer. She wouldn't make him wait, not because she was submitting to his demands but because she couldn't wait to wipe the smug look sitting on his face off.

"My answer is simple." She bent her lips into the broadest smile she could manage. "Go to hell."

CHAPTER TWO

"I DON'T KNOW why you went over there. You should've known Jasiri wasn't going to just give you his stake in the house."

Reigna narrowed her gaze, sending a stiff glare in her identical twin's direction. She had come to her sister's austere office that looked more like a lab with its white walls and furniture, not an ounce of color to be found except the identical brown beauty herself.

"What I should've known is that my twin was going to point out my flaws instead of supporting me in my anger against my trifling ex."

Regina, born two minutes after Reigna, with the exact same face and a completely opposite personality, was all logic, process, numbers, chemicals, and equations. Where Reigna was all fire and emotion, Regina was the twin that didn't let herself get led around by her finicky heart. It was a trait Reigna wished she possessed, especially after her meeting with Jasiri yesterday.

"Reigna, stop being dramatic. All I'm saying is you know how Jasiri is, how he always has been. Hell, I wasn't the sister sleeping with him and even I knew he wasn't going to honor your request after the way you threw dirt on his proposal."

Reigna glared harder, but just like before, her sister stared at her with not even the slightest bit of concern or compassion for her.

"Regina, I didn't throw dirt on his proposal. I told him I wasn't ready to get married."

"No," Regina shook her head as she pointed an accusing finger at Reigna. "You told him you didn't want to marry *him*."

Reigna huffed at her sister's penchant for remembering the slightest detail for everything.

"I was nervous, Regina. He surprised me in front of the entire Devereaux family, and with all those expectant eyes on me I just froze up. He never gave me a chance to explain that what I meant was that I wasn't ready to get married to anyone, not specifically him."

Reigna remembered that day as if it had happened mere moments ago. After two years of dating, Jasiri knelt with his bright smile, holding the largest diamond she'd ever seen, waiting expectantly for her yes. When it never came, he prodded her for an answer. Feeling trapped, she blurted out that she didn't want to marry him and ran from the room.

If there was any day she could take back, it would've been that one. Not that she would've changed her mind about the proposal, she wouldn't have. But she would've made sure Jasiri understood it had nothing to do with him and everything to do with the horrible example of marriage her parents gave her.

Backbiting, cheating, and physical, emotional, and verbal abuse, those were the relationship tools her parents had gifted her with. No matter how much she wanted to accept his proposal, she couldn't trap him in the vicious prison she knew marriage to be, not when she loved him so much.

Her sister rose from her desk, taking the open space next to Reigna on the couch.

"I know that, sister. But he doesn't. Jasiri is a proud man. You hurt his pride. Until you make that right, you'll never get him to sell you his share of the house."

Regina took her hand, lacing their fingers together. It was something they'd both done for as long as either of them could remember. Even though her sister rarely held pretty words for Regina's antics, she always knew how to make her feel protected and safe.

"Is the house worth all of this, Reigna? We

both know you can afford to buy a home any-where. Why do you have to own this one?"

Reigna slid down on the cushions, placing her head on her sister's shoulder. "Because we were happy in that house. We walked around Mom and Dad on pins and needles for so long. When she left, we were still afraid to even breathe the wrong way for fear she'd come back, and the nightmare would start all over again. It wasn't until we moved into that house after the divorce that Ace promised us we'd have nothing but happiness there. That we'd be safe."

"I know," Regina squeezed her hand lightly. "But is past happiness worth giving Jasiri what he wants? I love that house and all the memo-ries we had there. But I couldn't make the sac-rifice Jasiri is asking of you. Is this truly about how happy we were there?"

Reigna took in a shaky breath, and it was as if the dam of pain she'd been holding inside for nearly a week since they'd learned of their uncle's death began to crumble.

"I just miss Ace so much, Regina. He prom-ised me that he wouldn't leave me before I was ready."

"I know, sister. He promised me the same. I wasn't ready either."

Reigna curled into her sister's embrace, need-ing her strength to keep it together.

"We have to say goodbye to him today, Regina. The closer we get to the funeral, the more I just need to hold on to something that I shared with Uncle Ace. Is that so wrong?"

Regina placed a sweet kiss on her head and patted her cheek. "No, Reigna, there's nothing wrong with that at all. But you know what you're going to have to do to get it. You're either going to fight Jasiri in court, and our cousin Amara has already said it would be a fruitless pursuit. Or, you're going to have to become Mrs. Jasiri Adebesi for the next two years. So again, I must ask you if the house is worth that."

It was a fair question, and if she'd witnessed anyone else going through this situation, she'd probably ask the same. But she couldn't walk away from this house. It was the house where their uncle had brought love and stability into their lives. It was the house where Ace found her in her bedroom after her mother had left them, and when she asked if Ace was going to leave her too, he'd said, "I'll always be here for my babies. I'll fight the good Lord himself if he tries to take me before you're ready."

She'd held him to that promise, and he'd been there through all the ups and downs of her life. The only thing he'd ever asked her in return was that she would someday make the house a home again and fill it with joy and laughter the way it once had been.

She'd gladly agreed to that promise then. And as much as she wished like hell Ace hadn't put her in this situation, a promise was a promise, and she would keep it, no matter what she had to do to accomplish it.

"It's the only thing I have left of the man who loved us through some of the toughest times of our lives. I can't just walk away from this, Regina."

Her twin separated from their embrace and looked at her with clear eyes. "Then, I guess you have your answer."

Reigna managed a weak smile before she nodded. "I guess I do."

"Baba, how are you?"

Jasiri sat in his diplomatic limousine adorned with the flag of his nation and his princely coat of arms as he watched mourners filter into the large Baptist church on the corner.

"Mwana," King Omari crooned in the loving way he'd always done when he used the Swahili word for *son*. Jasiri's heart swelled at the sight of his father's smile and the clear sound of his voice. "I miss you, my boy."

The last time he'd seen the man in person, Omari had been lying in a hospital bed connected to tubes and machines as doctors worked tirelessly to bring his blood pressure down from near stroke levels.

Determined to keep his father alive and in good health, Jasiri had promised the ancestors right then and there that if they protected his father, he'd do everything in his power to remove the burden of the mantle of king from his head and simultaneously protect their descendants, the people of Nyeusi.

Jasiri shared a warm smile with the man. "Baba, things are moving along as expected."

It was the closest thing to the truth Jasiri could come up with. His father would not have sanctioned Jasiri's tactics into strong-arming Reigna into marrying him to make him eligible for the throne. No, he would not approve at all. That was yet another reason Jasiri was intentionally keeping the truth from his father.

"I was so happy when you told me you and Reigna had reconciled and she'd agreed to be your queen."

Agreed to be his queen? That was laughable. She'd have to first know Jasiri was royalty to know marrying him would make her queen of Nyeusi. A truth he had no intention of sharing until they were either in Nyeusian airspace or land for fear she'd run off. Jasiri was born into this life, and the thought of bearing such great responsibility on his shoulders nearly toppled him. He couldn't risk Reigna deciding it wasn't worth the bargain he was certain he could get her to make.

Even during their courtship, he had struggled with the secret of his birthright. The only way to survive the viciousness attached to royalty was to quickly discern who was with you for you or simply for what you could do for them.

He'd wanted to tell Reigna who he was from the first moment they met. But Sherard reminded him how unwise that was.

"People will use you and, by extension, the royal family to get what they want. Unchecked greed and desire will inevitably lead to scandal. Royal scandals are harmful, not just to the royals but the nation too. Look at how the paparazzi are always dogging the Windsors. You cannot be the cause of such shame and mockery being thrust upon the Nyeusian monarchy. Now some British people question whether they even need a monarchy. As the heir to the throne, you cannot give your people an opportunity to question if the monarchy is needed or not. Unless you are absolutely sure this person will protect you and protect the monarchy, you cannot risk sharing your identity with her."

Jasiri had heeded Sherard's wise counsel. He'd used the two years he'd spent with Reigna to prove to himself and his adviser that she could be trusted. They were in love, and he'd never felt safer than in her arms. He planned to tell her the truth after she'd accepted his proposal. But when Reigna refused his proposal, as outraged as he was that she'd turned him down, he'd never been more relieved that he'd followed Sherard's advice about revealing his identity. Now it was essential she remain unaware until he'd set every part of his plan in motion. He couldn't be seen as weak right now. To do so would amount to him handing the monarchy over to his uncle who only sought the throne to benefit himself, not the people.

"Is Reigna with you?"

"No," Jasiri answered honestly for the first time since he'd answered the video call. "She's with her family right now."

His father nodded. "Please give Reigna and the Devereauxs my sympathy on the passing of Ace. He was always a great friend to me, and if my doctors would allow me to travel, I'd be right there with you among the rest of her family to support her. She was very close to Ace. Every time I talked to the man, he'd go on and on about his babies. And Reigna was certainly included in that number. It tore him up to keep the secret of your royal status from her. Fortunately, as a man of great power, he understood the need for you to walk in the world as a normal man to get the sense of what the real world was like. He protected my son, and I will always be grateful to him for that."

The King dropped his eyes in reverence to his late friend before clearing his throat of the thickness of grief. There were few people in the world that his father held so dear, his expression of pain and loss was clear proof of that.

"This is a significant loss for her. You make sure to take good care of her during this difficult time."

Jasiri knew his father spoke the truth. Reigna and her sister Regina had been extremely close to Ace. He could only imagine how painful this day must be for her.

"Mwana," his father sat straighter, leaning toward the camera of his device. "You lost this woman once. Don't let inattention be the reason you lose her again. I'm serious when I say take good care of her. She will need you to get through this."

"Baba, I will be everything Reigna needs me to be right now."

His father's pride in him as a son and a man shone through the screen. Knowing he was lying to his father about the state of his relationship with Reigna and his position among the many mourners who would pay tribute to

Ace should have made Jasiri feel lower than a snake's belly slithering on the ground.

But if lying to his king and father was the only way to keep the man alive, then Jasiri would spin as many tales as necessary to keep King Omari happy and safe. Doing what needed to be done for the greater good was the responsibility of any king. And since Jasiri would be next to rule, he considered this charade practice for the sovereign he was about to become.

Marrying Reigna was the best thing he could do for his father, his country, and himself. Yes, marrying her would help him protect his father's health, stabilize the monarchy, and keep his father's line as the rightful monarchs of the nation. More importantly, however, marrying her meant he wouldn't be so distracted by love that he'd let his relationship rule him the way it had when he'd loved her.

Reigna's dismissal of him and his proposal had twisted him in knots for months. He'd barely been able to function, and his work as crown prince and ambassador of Nyeusi had suffered greatly. He'd been fortunate that Sherard had been there to cover for him, ensuring no harm resulted from the dereliction of Jasiri's duties. As king, he could not take that risk. That meant that the safest bet was for him to marry the woman who'd crushed his heart and make certain he'd never love anyone else again, not even her.

The sight of an elegant woman dressed in black with large black sunglasses headed toward his car caught his attention, making him brace for battle.

"Baba, Reigna's here. I must go."

"Very well, son." With a brief nod, his father ended the call, and his phone screen went dark. Before his security detail could knock on the glass and ask his permission to let her near the car, Jasiri opened the window just far enough to give the guard an affirmative wave of his hand.

Soon, the door opened, and Reigna was sliding inside, pulling her sunglasses off before locking gazes with him.

"Hello, Reigna. You have my deepest sympathy."

She held up a hand, her eyes narrowing into sharp slits as she glared at him.

"Spare me the platitudes, Jasiri. I know they're not genuine."

His body tensed at her words. He wasn't sure why, but it almost bothered him that she didn't believe him.

"Well, if it's to be that way, let me get straight to it, then. Why are you in my car, Reigna?"

He waited patiently, refusing to push her.

Reigna tended to bolt when she was cornered, and he needed her thinking clearly if his plan had a prayer of working.

"I'm here to accept your terms, Jasiri." Her words were as sharp as her glare. "I'll marry you and live in your country for two years so you can take over your father's office. But the moment two years is up I will be on the first thing smoking back to New York with the deed that declares me the only owner of my family's home."

Jasiri sat back in the soft leather of his seat, lifting an eyebrow in acknowledgment.

"You've made a wise decision, Reigna."

"I've made the only decision that you've given me."

"True," he replied. "And as long as you remember that, this will work out perfectly."

She watched Jasiri as he leaned forward, as if he were making sure she could see his face clearly. He took hold of her hand, sliding the same large diamond onto her ring finger that he'd offered her two years ago when he'd proposed. The heft of it, both physically and emotionally, caused her to flex her fingers. It was proof of their agreement. She was getting exactly what she wanted and keeping her promise to her late uncle while simultaneously helping

Jasiri protect his father. It was a simple business transaction. But as her chest tightened as she stared at this outward sign of their engagement, she couldn't escape the fact that the ring felt more like a shackle than a piece of expensive jewelry.

"If you try to double-cross me, Reigna," he said in a deep, low grumble, "I promise you will live to regret the day you laid eyes on me." It was a warning. One she knew she couldn't ignore.

"Too late for that, Jasiri." She swallowed, trying hard to push her visible anger down. "I already do."

CHAPTER THREE

REIGNA LOOKED AROUND the hallowed walls of Brown Memorial Baptist Church. The service had been going on for an hour, and she'd refused to look directly at Ace's casket the entire time she'd been there.

This place had always been filled with joy and exuberance as people, including the Devereaux family, had worshipped and communed in both brotherly love and their faith.

Funerals were no exception to this. They were celebrations of life, home-going services where those that remained worked through their grief with uplifting songs that told of going up yonder to be with their creator, and spiritual dances that seemed to electrify everyone in attendance.

Inside this sacred place, even in pain, the masses could find momentary joy.

Reigna tried her hardest to remember that. To remember those memories where love and joy flowed so easily from Ace to her and to her sister. To sing along with the choir in joy as the church jubilantly celebrated Ace's life and contributions to this community. To not let the grief welling up inside her smother her.

She sat bookended between Jasiri and Regina on the long wooden pew. Her cousin Stephan sat in the same position on the other side of the pew with his husband Carter holding him up on one side and their daughter Naveah stroking his large hand with her small one on the other.

What she wouldn't give to have what those two men shared, a family, a built-in comforter for when the world was on your shoulders. Would she have had that by now if she'd accepted Jasiri's proposal? Would he have been her shelter in this tumultuous storm?

She knew what the comfort of a loved one felt like. Her entire childhood, Ace had been that person. Her mind traveled back to the day her sister, their father, and Reigna moved into the beautiful brownstone house around the corner from the Devereaux Manor mansion Ace resided in.

Her father and mother's divorce was finalized, and Ace allowed her father Johnathan to move in with his eight-year-old twin daughters.

Regina, of course, had found a way to bury her pain in her schoolwork. Reigna, on the other hand, could hardly function with this new existence she was being forced to live. She could still remember sitting on the bench by the back windows, looking out into the concrete backyard of their new Brooklyn home when the warm voice of her favorite uncle had surrounded her.

"Hey, little one. Why so sad?"

Reigna hadn't been able to bring herself to turn around. At least if she kept her eyes fixed on the cold concrete, no one could see her tears.

Her young mind hadn't been able to articulate all the big feelings she was experiencing, so she'd shrugged her shoulders, then turned to her great-uncle and said, *"Because we don't have a family anymore. Mommy's gone and Daddy's at work all the time. It's just people Daddy hired to take care of us."*

Those words had ushered in another round of jagged crying, but this time, instead of leaving her crying alone, Ace had wrapped her up in his arms and said, *"As long as you have me, you'll have family, little one."*

He must've seen the doubt creeping into her little furrowed brow because he'd pulled back to make sure she could see the sincerity in his eyes.

"I promise I'll come see about you and your

sister regularly. We'll make as many happy memories as you can stand in this place."

Her tears had stopped as his words fostered hope to bloom inside of her.

"You promise, Uncle Ace?"

"I sure do, baby. But I need you to make me a promise too."

Hungry for the attention and affection of a father figure, Reigna had nodded.

"First, I need you to dry your tears. Because when I come to see my girls, all I wanna see is them happy."

Reigna had quickly wiped her face with the backs of her hands and did her best to hold a shaky smile in place.

"Second..." His eyes had sparkled with the love and joy only an elder could manage to muster for the younger generations in their family. *"I need you to promise me that when you're all grown-up, you will pour joy and laughter into this house too, so the next generation of Devereauxs can be happy."*

Reigna hadn't understood what that meant, really. She hadn't exactly been sure how she was gonna put joy and laughter into a bag and then pour it all over this fancy new house Uncle Ace let them live in. But she figured that must be something she could learn how to do as a grown-up, right?

She'd nodded enthusiastically, ready to promise this man anything, including her favorite Kenya and Kiana dolls, if it meant having someone who cared about her because of her and not because they were getting paid to.

He had smiled down at her, calming every insecurity that had been sewn inside of her by her parents.

"Do we have a deal, little one?"

She'd tilted her head as she looked up at him before speaking again.

"Almost."

Ace had chuckled, his shoulders shaking as his laughter filled the room. She hadn't been quite sure what he was laughing at, she'd just known that she wanted to hear more of it. Because she didn't feel so alone when the grownups around her laughed.

"You gotta promise that you're never gonna leave us like Mommy and Daddy."

He'd grabbed her to him, hugging her so tight she'd thought he might squeeze the air out of her like a balloon.

"I'll always be here for my babies as long as they need me. I'll fight the good Lord himself if he tries to take me before you're ready."

The feel of Jasiri's arm sliding across the back of the pew pulled her from her living memory, tearing away the one reprieve from the pain of Ace's loss since she'd learned of his passing.

"Are you holding up okay? Would you like me to have one of my men bring you a bottle of water?"

His voice in her ear and the inevitable way he had to lean into her in her current position felt like relief and warmth, and pain and sorrow all at the same time. If he were anyone else offering her this small kindness, she would've graciously accepted. But Jasiri wasn't anyone else. He was the man who was blackmailing her to keep the one piece of Ace she had left.

For that reason alone, she wouldn't be weak in front of him, not for any reason. Not even to grieve Ace.

"No, thank you." She managed to whisper those words, even as the thicket of emotion from glimpsing the black lacquered casket at the front of the church that held her beloved uncle's earthly form.

"I just need to get through the rest of this service, and I'll be fine."

His knowing gaze said he didn't believe a word of what she'd just said. But he nodded in acknowledgment, keeping whatever he was thinking behind those warm brown eyes that seemed to call to her.

"Reigna, it's okay to not be okay tonight."

His words sounded so sincere. She couldn't shake the feeling, though, that this was all an act. Yes, he'd held Ace in great esteem, but was that regard enough to have him put down his battlements for a time just to comfort her?

She refused to risk it and make a fool of herself yet again when it came to this man that was sitting all too close for her comfort.

Between the renewed ache covering her heart after her mind had brought her to the present and the anger Jasiri's mere presence invoked, those same mix of confused emotions that filled her up when she was eight seemed to resurface with a vengeance.

Her thoughts clattered around her head, and her chest tightened making it difficult to breathe.

"I bet you'd love that." Her teeth were clenched, and her mouth was flat. She was leaning into him while the choir sang the upbeat "When We All Get to Heaven" and, with the hand-clapping that accompanied them, no one could hear her but Jasiri.

"Wouldn't you? To see me broken and weak?" She struggled to take a deep breath before she spoke again. "I won't give you the satisfaction."

She returned her vision to the front of the church and watched as the choir, all decked out in white robes, began to sway to the slower transition notes the organist played. As the choir sang the heartfelt lyrics of "Order My Steps in Your Word," Reigna could feel what little resolve she'd managed to hold on to splinter as her chest tightened and her heart began to beat like a loud drum in her chest.

Not now. Oh, God, not now. Not in front of all these people, not in front of Jasiri.

She held her hand to her chest, trying to anchor herself in the moment and not the overwhelming grief suffocating her or the icy panic she could feel tightening her muscles and spiraling up her spine.

She stood up quickly. When her sister stood with her, she shook her head. Yes, they were twins. But this, these moments where her body and mind refused to work in harmony, Reigna wouldn't allow even the one she'd shared a womb with to witness her like this.

Her body trembled with fear, and as much as she told her legs to move, they refused to listen.

She grabbed the back of the pew, hoping to borrow its strength to keep herself upright.

"Reigna?"

Jasiri's voice broke through the raucous noise ringing in her head, disrupting her tumultuous thoughts.

She opened her mouth, but no words came

out. Something flashed across his eyes that she couldn't recognize. Was it fear, panic, concern? She didn't know. Her own senses were overstimulated, making it hard for her to make sense of the world around her.

She closed her eyes, taking in a slow shaky breath and fighting to push all the racket out of her head. Goodness, she was so angry. She was angry at Jasiri for putting her in this position. She was angry at Ace for leaving her. But most of all, she was furious at herself for forfeiting this round to Jasiri so easily.

She tried so hard to be quiet. To not draw attention to herself, to be strong in her pain, to bind the ache that demanded to be set free. She didn't want to let the enemy sitting next to her see her so destroyed.

The problem, however, was that she *was* destroyed. She was wrecked.

She tried to take another breath, but her lungs seized, and then she knew she'd either have to swallow her pride or die where should stood.

And wouldn't that be the story running through the gossip rags? *Heiress and Greatniece of the Brooklyn Mogul Ace Devereaux Collapses Dead at His Funeral.*

She locked eyes with Jasiri, and he stood immediately. He asked no questions. He wrapped a strong arm around her waist that made her feel anchored and safe.

Before she could grab on to his arm like the lifeline it was, she felt herself being lifted.

"I've got you," he whispered in her ear and the tightness in her chest seemed to ease just a bit. "Just hold on."

She buried her face in his chest, hoping to preserve even a sliver of her dignity. But her traitorous heart just wouldn't let her hold it all in.

By the time she felt solid wood beneath her again, her body was a trembling mess and her fight for air was making her dizzy.

She felt a familiar hand at the center of chest pressing hard enough that she focused on it but not hard enough to bring harm.

"Breathe with me, Reigna."

Jasiri placed one of her hands atop his on her chest and took her remaining hand and cradled it against his chest.

"Let's do it together. Slow, deep breath in."

He began calmly, and she tried her best to follow.

"Slow, deep breath out."

Again, she tried to follow him. She tried to close her eyes and the panic began to strengthen like a powerful storm out on the water.

"Eyes on me, Reigna. Eyes on me."

He'd said those words before. Usually when she was so blissed out from their lovemaking that she could hardly see straight. He would utter those words, demanding she be present for every moment of pleasure they gave to each other.

She obediently opened her eyes and continued to follow his commands to take slow, deep breaths in and out.

When her head stopped spinning and his strong features came into sharpened view, she looked around to find them in the near-empty vestibule where he had her huddled in a corner while his security team stood by the entrances and windows. He knelt before her, pulling a silk black handkerchief from his front pocket and tentatively handed it to her.

"Reigna." He said her name with such care, as if it were something delicate he needed to protect. "I know that you despise me, hate me even for what I'm making you do."

He wasn't wrong; there was no denying it.

"But tonight, let us call a ceasefire to our personal battle. For tonight and tomorrow, while you must bear your grief publicly, just let it go. Let me pay my respects to a great man by helping you carry this burden."

She trembled with the need to both fight and acquiesce simultaneously. How she ached to let him take this away from her, even for a second.

She shook her head. "Jasiri, I..."

He cupped her cheek, softly stroking the wet skin beneath his thumb, and in this moment of despair, it felt like a life raft.

"Just for tonight and tomorrow, Reigna. Just for tonight and tomorrow. When these services end, you can go right back to hating me... I promise."

The soft timbre of his voice had her nodding, and before her next tear could fall, he sat beside her, pulling her into his warm embrace, and she let go just like she had all those years ago when Ace had comforted her in an almost identical way.

She knew she would come to regret this. She knew her momentary weakness would cost her in the end. But for tonight and tomorrow, she would use the shoulder he was offering and just let go.

As he held her tightly against him as her body shook with hurt, a small voice whispered in her ear.

Maybe he's not the devil incarnate. Maybe there's a tiny bit of the old Jasiri still in there somewhere.

Jasiri watched Reigna as she circulated through the room tending to guests and family at Ace's repast. He'd been at her side for both the private and public services, and he'd done what any loving fiancé would do for the woman he loved in her time of need.

But he didn't love Reigna, not anymore.

This fact made it even harder for him to understand why it was so easy for him to slip back into his old role as her protector, her rock.

In their time together, he'd seen Reigna angry, happy, passionate, and so many other loud emotions that she never tried to hide. But in that sanctuary, he had seen absolute panic in her eyes.

How had he not known? They'd been so close. Shouldn't he have known if this was a problem for her before? Or was this just grief-induced? Had the funeral and the pressure Jasiri was placing on her just been too much?

He reconciled his warring thoughts by telling himself he was just doing what any other human being would do. Although his position in life sometimes meant he had to be calculating, he wasn't heartless. He didn't revel in her pain. Well, he reveled in annoying her and getting under her skin. Call him juvenile, but her frustration with him, especially when he outmaneuvered her, it felt glorious. He was a petty prince, so sue him.

But even his pettiness had its limits. There was no way he could sit next to her, immovable as stone, and watch her crumble under the weight of her pain. Besides, his mother would've had his hide if he had. There was no way a son of hers would be anything but a gentleman in that situation. Not if he knew what was good for him.

"Jasiri."

At the sound of his name, he turned to find Regina Devereaux coming toward him. His protection detail was all around the room, blending in with the other mourners but giving him just enough space to interact with others. He tipped his head to the head of his security, and the man moved seamlessly, letting Regina slip through.

"Regina, I'm sorry for your loss."

Regina took a steadying breath, gently smoothing the sleek hair she had pulled into a severe bun.

Jasiri had never had trouble telling the two sisters apart. Yes, they were identical down to the placement of their beauty marks right above their lip. But to him, Regina's cool logic and Reigna's fire and passion had always distinguished one woman from the other.

"Thanks, Jasiri. I really appreciate you coming. Especially considering all that's going on between you and my sister right now."

"So you know about our arrangement?"

Regina scoffed as if his question were the most ridiculous thing she'd ever heard.

"Of course I know about it. She's my twin. We don't keep secrets from each other."

The corners of his mouth curled into a genuine smile. He'd missed Regina's no-nonsense attitude. Unlike most of the people Jasiri had to engage with in his official capacity, Regina never pulled any punches. What you saw was most definitely what you got. You never had to worry about where you stood with her. She would tell you.

"I guess this is the point where you voice your disapproval."

She folded her arms across her chest and leveled her gaze at him.

"The only thing I disapprove of is the way you went about enlisting her help. You didn't have to threaten her with the thing she needs most…especially now."

"I had no choice, Regina. My father's life depends on her agreement."

"I understand that." He could see a glimpse of pain cascade over her face, but before he could acknowledge it, it was gone. Where Reigna wore her pain outwardly, Regina kept everything inside. He almost felt sorry for her in that moment.

"After losing the man who was a father figure to us, I understand your fear of losing your father. I would've moved heaven and earth to keep Ace here if I could've."

She dipped her head for a moment before clearing her throat and continuing.

"If I understand your plight, Reigna does too. You didn't have to blackmail her. She would've done it because it's the right thing to do. She would never want anyone else to bear this pain like we are. All you had to do was ask."

He glanced over to where Reigna was standing, needing to know where she was in the room.

"I did ask, and she refused."

Regina shook her head matter-of-factly.

"No, you demanded. Just because you phrased that demand as a request doesn't mean it was one."

She had him there. In his defense, he was the next ruler of a nation. The ability to command had been drilled into him from his childhood.

"You've always been a decent man who treated my sister well. Make sure that remains the case when you take her to your homeland."

She plastered a broad smile on her face before she picked an imaginary piece of lint off his lapel.

"Because I might be too pretty to go to jail for busting a diplomat's head to the white meat.

But if you hurt my sister, there's not a military or government official alive that will keep me off you."

She said it in jest, but Jasiri believed every word she spoke. Knowing how determined and capable the Devereaux sisters were, he was certain she could get away with it too.

"I know Reigna hurt you by turning down your proposal. But if you spend less time digging into your pride and more time talking to her instead, I think this little deal the two of you have could be beneficial to you both in ways neither of you have considered."

Regina gave him a reassuring smile before she stepped away from him, leaving him to realize how much he'd missed out on in having her as a sister-in-law.

Was she right? Could he really have avoided this tension if he'd just genuinely asked for Reigna's help?

It was too late to worry about that now. The die was cast, and there was just too much to lose to risk it to chance. But perhaps Regina was right. Perhaps he could relax his manner around her. Make things less formal and rigid between them.

At just that moment, Reigna's cold gaze met his from across the room, and her disapproving glare halted any idea he had of relaxing his demeanor around her. Reigna was a woman out for blood, and he'd be damned if it was his father's that spilled as a result of his inability to make Reigna live up to her end of their unorthodox bargain.

"All right, then." He tipped his head toward her. "I guess the truce is off."

CHAPTER FOUR

HER LANDLINE RANG, which signaled it was probably her doorman calling. Anyone else knew to call her on her cell.

"Hello, Ms. Devereaux. This is Ralph at the front desk."

She'd called it.

"Hi, Ralph. How may I help you?"

"There's a Mr. Sherard and he's here with four rather large men accompanying him. He's asking for permission to come up. Should I buzz them in?"

Reigna pictured Sherard and who she imagined must be part of Jasiri's security detail standing in front of the poor, elderly man who'd stood at the front of her building since it was erected decades ago, terrifying him with their mean faces and serious body language.

"I know who he is, Ralph. Please let the five gentlemen up. They'll probably be another set of people following them. If one of them is a Jasiri Adebesi, please send them up."

Reigna stepped away from the mountain of clothing strewn across her bed. Relieved to ignore the pile, if only for a few moments. She made her way to the front door of her penthouse to let Sherard and his goons in.

As soon as she opened the door, Sherard and two of his four men filled the space while the remaining two stood vigil on either side of the entryway.

"Sherard, it's a bit early for your secret-agent-man routine. What do you want?"

"The ambassador is waiting to come upstairs. Before he can, his team will need to do a security sweep of your abode."

When they'd first begun dating, this routine rattled her. She'd never dated a diplomat before. She'd had no idea they required so much security, especially from a little island most people hadn't heard of. Now she was seasoned and knew what to expect, so she stepped aside, standing at the door with Sherard as he and the men started the sweep.

When they'd finished, Sherard directed the two security specialists at the door to remain while he instructed the other men to retrieve Jasiri.

"Did you put him up to this, Sherard?"

He turned around, meeting her gaze for the first time since he'd arrived at her apartment.

Sherard was a tall, solid man. An elder statesman that moved with grace and exuded cool detachment almost as well as her sister Regina.

His posture was perfect, and his manners impeccable. Even when he was being glib, it was so polite you couldn't tell if you wanted to curse him out or curtsy in response.

His skin was a deep brown. High cheekbones and full lips with a smooth clean-shaven face, and only gray patches at his temples to hint at the decades he had on her and Jasiri.

He was Jasiri's Alfred Pennyworth, always in the background, always taking care of Jasiri, and always working out a plan to protect the young diplomat.

"That is a safe assumption, Ms. Devereaux. It is of the utmost importance that the young Adebesi fulfill this requirement to spare his father and our country."

"Is one ambassador really so important to a nation?"

He straightened his shoulders, as if they weren't already straight enough to rest a platter of wineglasses safely on them.

"Yes, Ms. Devereaux. *This* ambassador is."

His words were straightforward, but there was something about his delivery, about the way he stressed the word *this* that raised the baby hairs on the back Reigna's neck. She ignored the prickles of trepidation crawling over her skin and chalked it up to the annoyance this man and his stiff and unapproachable demeanor had always stirred in her. Even when she and Jasiri were dating, she'd always had to resist the urge to roll her eyes whenever she came in contact with this pretentious traveling butler.

Before she could respond, her front door was opened by one of the men standing outside, and Jasiri entered.

"Reigna." He took her in slowly as if he were assessing her, making sure she was all right.

She fought not to shrink under his gaze. She'd been weak enough in front of him. She wouldn't embarrass herself any further.

"Sherard, I wish to speak to my bride alone."

"Sir, that's not protocol."

"Sherard, I do not—"

"It's okay, Jasiri. We can go to my home office to speak in private. Your men can remain inside the apartment."

If Jasiri was as important as Sherard seemed to think he was, Reigna thought it better to be safe than sorry, even though she couldn't imagine someone entering her fourteenth-floor penthouse.

Jasiri nodded, and she led the way to her office. She hadn't changed anything about her apartment since he'd last been here two years ago. So, she wasn't surprised to see him follow her easily along the corridors in the spacious apartment.

Her office was a monochrome ivory dream. Her walls, her desk and chair, the thick, plush rug, all the technological accessories, and furniture were ivory. Everything looked like heaven had exploded in this one room. There were splashes of beiges and browns throughout to bring just a pop of color to it, including the large beige-and-brown rendering of President Nelson Mandela, President Barack Obama, Dr. Martin Luther King Jr., and El-Hajj Malik El-Shabazz, better known as Malcolm X, sitting comfortably, smiling and conversing as joy and respect spread between the four of them.

"What a time it would've been if those four great men had been gifted the chance to sit and talk about the greatness of our people across the diaspora."

Warmth spread through her, making her lips curve into an involuntary smile.

"Ace used to say the same thing."

Jasiri gave a brief tip of his head in acknowledgment. "I know. I've heard him say it multiple times. He had great admiration for those pillars in our community."

Admiration was a mild word to describe the limitless pride and esteem Ace had had for those four men. He was in awe of their brilliance, their courage, and their commitment to the diaspora.

"You know," Reigna smiled as she remembered and then spoke the very words Ace had spoken to her several times over, "he supported all of them during their individual movements. He walked with Malcolm and Martin during the sixties Civil Rights Movement. Malcolm and Martin might not have agreed with each other's methods, but they both respected Ace and his respective love for each of them."

Jasiri kept his eyes on the painting as if he was committing each stroke to memory. She didn't blame him: the power the imagined moment captured was enough to captivate anyone who had a passable understanding of who these four leaders were and what they meant to Black people.

She walked closer to the wall, running a gingerly finger across the canvas as if touching it somehow allowed her to touch the greatness of the history depicted in the artist's strokes.

"He visited Mandela frequently while he was imprisoned," she continued. "He was there when he was released. And when Obama ran for president, Ace was so proud of him. He stood on the stage for President Obama's victory speech, crying like a newborn baby. Barrack Obama was the one miracle he'd never thought he'd live to see."

He stepped across the room until he was standing shoulder to shoulder with her.

"If you ask me," Jasiri offered, "the painting is missing one illustrious man. Ace should've been included in this imagined meeting of the greats too."

Reigna closed her eyes, not because grief was threatening to overwhelm her right now. No, it was because hearing someone else talk about Ace, painting him in the exact same greatness she'd always seen him cloaked in, felt warm and inviting.

She turned around, ready to share a smile with Jasiri when she remembered why he was there. As much as they both admired Ace, she couldn't let that be the reason she let down her guard when it came to this man.

"So I assume you came to bring details of our trip to Nyeusi."

She could tell her cool words had broken whatever spell reminiscing about her uncle had surrounded them. Part of her wished she could take her words back and just stay in that moment of kinship and peace between them. Jasiri may have been Ace's friend, but he wasn't hers. If she were going to survive this ordeal unscathed, she would have to remember that.

"I came to check up on you. To see how you are doing."

She could see the concern marring the smooth skin of his forehead.

"I'm fine, Jasiri. It was noth—"

"How long have you suffered from panic attacks?"

"Jasiri, you're imagin—"

He waved his hand, cutting off the lie she was gearing up to tell.

"I know what I saw, Reigna. You knew what was happening to you, even if you couldn't stop it. That tells me the funeral wasn't the first time this occurred. How long?"

Her heavy sigh filled the silence of the room. She didn't know if it was resignation to admit to his observations or relief to be able to speak the words to someone else.

"I haven't had one since I was a child." Her voice was soft as she met his gaze. "Ace was the only one who knew."

"Your parents and your sister didn't know?"

She pulled her bottom lip between her teeth, her tell that she was feeling out of her depth.

"I hid them. I'd lock myself in my room, run to my en suite bathroom and run the shower while I worked through them. They only ever flared up when my parents were fighting. Regina and I always ran to our own separate corners when that happened. Like neither of us wanted to acknowledge the hell that was being raised in our home."

She sat down on her large ivory couch and waved her hand, silently inviting Jasiri to sit.

"Ace was visiting for dinner when my parents started going at it. Both Regina and I took off to our respective rooms. He must have gone to Regina's room first, because it took him a few minutes before he knocked on my door. But when I didn't answer, he panicked and used his pocketknife to unlock it."

She twiddled with the hem of her dress, needing something to do with her shaky hands. She cleared her throat and continued in the same matter-of-fact tone she'd been using since he'd brought the topic up.

"He found me in the throes of an attack. Without the slightest bit of hesitation, he sat on the floor next to me, pulled me into his arms, and cradled me until my heart stopped racing and I could breathe again. The next day, he made my parents an offer. If they'd divorce and my father agreed to the three of us moving into one of Ace's houses, Ace would pay them five million dollars each and allow my dad to live in luxury rent-free."

"And your attacks?"

The gentle, yet firm tone of his voice was generously seasoned with expectation. She should've revolted against it. None of this was his business, especially now when he was forcing her into a marriage that neither of them wanted to be in.

But beneath his calm, she could see his entire attention focused on her, and in some strange way, she felt almost comforted. He was listening to her with concern.

"Once Ace became our de facto parent and removed us from all that turmoil, they never came back. Not until…"

"Ace's funeral."

She didn't have to reply. They both knew he was right. She looked up at him expecting to see pity or glee staring back at her. What she wasn't prepared to see was compassion.

"I can't imagine what my own response to that kind of trauma would've been. Thank God for Ace's care. Reigna, I—"

"Jasiri," she held up her hand to stop him. Whatever he was about to say wouldn't change what they each needed from each other in that moment. At this point, they were only a means to an end. That's all they could be.

"I don't need you feeling sorry for me. You care too much about your father to let me out of this ridiculous deal, so save whatever pretty words you think would make me feel better, and let's get on with this. What did you come here to tell me?"

He straightened his shoulders before he spoke again, tucking whatever concern she'd seen in his eyes safely away.

"We need to marry on Nyeusian soil. It must happen quickly, as in a matter of days. Can you be packed and ready to leave by the end of the week? Will you be able to scrounge up a witness by then? If not, I can just appoint someone."

"Regina would be my obvious choice as a witness." She answered coolly as if she were just talking about something unimportant. Even though this marriage was fake, it had very real consequences. That made it feel like they shouldn't be talking about it so casually.

"I know this isn't a real marriage. But it kind of feels wrong to get married without my family beside me. At the very least, I feel like I should have my sister present."

"Good," he responded. "We'll bring her along, then."

If only her life were that simple. She fell back into the cushions of her sofa and sighed.

"I'm not sure that will be possible. She has a lot on her plate, now that I'm leaving. I don't know if she'll be able to leave the country right now just to watch me get fake-married."

"Reigna," he said as he stood and walked to her office door, "our relationship may be a lie, but this marriage will be very real, legal, and binding."

The intensity in his voice made her spine stiffen, forcing her to stand as if she were preparing for an attack. What exactly did he mean by *real, legal, and binding*?

As if he were reading her thoughts, he lifted a brow as he let his gaze sweep from her head to feet and back again. "I've never had a woman in my bed who didn't expressly agree to be there, so you can wipe that worried look off your face. My expectation of this marriage is this. There will only be two people in this partnership, you and me. Infidelity is not an option on either of our parts. Are we clear, Reigna?"

Those words poured over her like fire on ice, melting something inside of her.

"Was that some sort of an accusation?"

He pushed his hands inside of his dress paints, creating a more imposing figure in front of her office door.

"It's been two years since we've been together, Reigna. I don't assume you've been living like a nun since then. Whoever may have been in your life up until this moment is irrelevant to me. Just know that whether we consummate this marriage or not, there will be no other men in your life until we are divorced. Are we clear?"

The chill his words had filled her with was giving way to her rising anger. She hated this version of Jasiri, the man who expected to have his orders followed when he spoke. He'd never shown his head while they were together. But from the moment she'd rejected his proposal, he always seemed to be present.

"Please don't talk to me like I'm one of your little minions. Remember, I'm helping you get what you want too."

His jaw ticked, and the immature child in her did a little victory dance in her head. If he wanted to act like a dictator, she'd check him every chance she could.

Whatever was running through his head, he must've decided to forgo speaking it because he reached inside of his jacket pocket and pulled out what looked like folded legal papers instead.

"I've had our prenuptial agreement drawn up. Have your lawyers check it over. Seeing as this marriage is happening so quickly, my lawyers suggest that we both film a declaration that neither of us is signing the document under duress. I've already filmed mine and signed the document. All that awaits is your signature, and we can get married."

Efficient and direct. That was always Jasiri. It shouldn't surprise her that he would carry out the process of their marriage the same way.

"I'll try to figure out our dilemma of having your sister present. I'll call when I have everything set up."

With a brief nod, he opened her office door. She stayed rooted to her spot as she listened to his footsteps, joined by those of his entourage, clicked on her hardwood floors in the halls and living room before she heard her front door close with a resolute click.

This was really happening. She was marrying her ex, Jasiri Adebesi. All it had taken was Ace dying and Jasiri's father nearly dying to bring it about.

CHAPTER FIVE

REIGNA WATCHED AS the limousine rolled through the gates of the Nyeusian embassy, and her chest tightened with just the slightest bit of concern. While she'd been at the consulate in Brooklyn many times throughout the course of their relationship and recently when she'd barged into Jasiri's office to call him out on his BS the moment she'd learned that Ace had willed him half of her family home, she realized now that she'd never been *here*.

The wide and high iron gates reminded her that this place was beyond her power and her privilege as an American citizen. Knowing what she was here to do made the hairs at the back of her neck stand at attention, as if someone were walking over her grave.

She was marrying the ambassador of Nyeusi beyond these gates and for all intents and purposes had stepped onto Nyeusi soil to do so.

Is past happiness worth giving Jasiri what he wants?

Her sister's words echoed in her head, each reverberation of her voice shaking Reigna's confidence in the wisdom of her accepting Jasiri's terms.

What the absolute hell had she been thinking to do this? Regina was right: she could buy any house she wanted. It didn't have to be that one. She didn't have to essentially sell herself to Jasiri to gain ownership of a home. She could just walk away.

But then the memory of Ace's black casket being lowered into the cold ground played behind her eyes as if she were standing there again, reliving the horror and the pain, and she knew she couldn't just walk away. It wasn't about having a house. It was about having a piece of the father figure she'd loved and lost. A piece she could keep with her forever, despite him being gone.

"Madam," the detached voice interrupted the troubling train of her thoughts, forcing her to remember where she was and what she was here to do. She met the gaze of the driver looking at her through the lowered privacy glass. "They're waiting for you inside. Are you ready?"

Reigna sat straight in her seat, making sure to still herself. She might question her own sanity in doing this, but no one in this embassy, including Jasiri himself, would know she was anything but strong and confident. It didn't matter if her insides felt like a bowl of wobbly jelly. It didn't matter if her mind kept asking her if it was wise to get this deeply involved with a man who'd caused so much havoc in her life. She would not let Jasiri be the thing that stopped her from honoring her promise to Ace and to herself. This was her heritage, and as she'd told her sister, Regina, it was well worth the cost.

Meeting the questioning gaze of the driver, she put on her Gemini Queens CEO smile and said, "I was born ready."

She watched as people she assumed were embassy staff lined up on the stairs leading to the front doors. When the driver opened her door, she placed one sleek Louboutin heel on the pavement and then the other, standing to her full height with her shoulders back, removing any doubt from anyone who looked at her that she was a self-made woman who owned every place she stepped inside of.

She shoved the last bit of uncertainty she had to the pit of her stomach and focused on each step, smiling along the way up the stairs until she was met by Sherard in the foyer.

"Welcome, Ms. Devereaux. Let me take you to your quarters."

As always, Sherard's words were short and

to the point. She followed him, taking in the large spacious foyer adorned with dark wood paneling that screamed luxury and understated opulence. The upstairs was much of the same. Thick, plush carpeting that silenced her stiletto heels covered the expansive hall. When they reached the end of it, Sherard opened the door and ushered her in.

When she stepped inside, there were two women and a man dressed in black with their hands positioned behind their backs. "Jenna, Asha, and Deshawn are here to get you ready," Sherard informed her. "The ceremony starts in exactly two hours. I will return for you and bring you downstairs for the ceremony. Should you need anything, pick up any telephone and dial one to call me. Everything you need should be here in your suite."

She gave him a brief nod to acknowledge him before he exited the room. When she turned around and saw the strange faces staring back at her, she doubted very seriously everything she needed was here as Sherard had said. How could that be true when her sister wasn't standing in front of her with her signature, no-nonsense scowl she always donned whenever they both knew Reigna was about to do something reckless that was going to land her in hot water?

"Are you having second thoughts? Because

if you are, I've already figured out an escape route through the basement."

Reigna's heart thudded against her chest as she followed the sound of the familiar voice to a doorway she hadn't seen when she'd walked in. There, in all her surly glory was Regina, her identical twin, standing with her arms folded across her chest.

Reigna ignored the three strangers, walking over to her sister and grabbing her into a fierce hug that nearly made the woman stumble back into the room. Happy to see her sister but aware they weren't alone, Reigna closed the door to what a quick glance told her was a bedroom before turning back to her sister.

"What are you doing here, Regina?"

"The question isn't why am I here," Regina replied, "but why didn't you tell me this was going down today? I had to get a call from that blowhard of a fiancé of yours telling me my sister needed me to stand up for her at her wedding."

Shame forced Reigna to drop her eyes from her sister's gaze. It was one of the difficulties of having an identical twin. When the same eyes you saw in the mirror were taking you to task, it made you feel even worse about yourself.

"Regina," Reigna huffed, "because of me, everything at work is being thrown in your lap.

That, and I know you don't necessarily agree with my decision. I didn't feel right asking you to take part in this knowing why all this is happening. Besides, the original plan was for the wedding to take place on Nyeusi. I didn't think you could get away for that."

"That was your first mistake," Regina responded. "Thinking."

Reigna smiled, knowing whatever came next out of her matter-of-fact twin's mouth was either going to burn her britches or make her laugh. Probably some combination of the two if she knew her sister. And she did.

"I'm the brainy twin. How about you leave all the thinking to me? You're the twin with all the heart. Your heart is telling you this is the right thing to do. Your heart has never led you wrong, Reigna. Trust it. Trust *me* when I tell you nobody has your back ten toes down like I do. I don't care about the circumstances. My sister is getting married today. There isn't a devil in hell that could keep me from standing by her side. Not even a foreign dignitary with all his diplomatic powers."

For the first time since all of this began, Reigna felt reassured. Her nerves stopped shaking as her sister's words soothed her. Regina was right. All Reigna had to do to make this work was trust her heart.

"I love you, sister," Reigna crooned as she pulled Regina into another hug.

"Of course you do," Reigna answered. "I'm the best."

Reigna stared down at the large diamond engagement ring, now accompanied by an eternity band, on her finger. Three hours ago, she'd married Jasiri in a small ceremony in the foyer of the embassy with an officiant and with her sister and Sherard as witnesses. After the businesslike ceremony where they'd answered in the affirmative in all the right places, they'd had a lovely brunch with her sister, and then they were off to a private airport and heading for Nyeusi.

"Why did you do it?"

Reigna said the words as she kept looking down at the wedding ring Jasiri had placed there.

"Why did I do what?" His voice was strong but soft, reminding her of the many times they'd been in a room alone talking without looking at one another.

Back then, it was because they were so in tune, they didn't need to see each other to know what the other was thinking or saying. Now… now she wasn't so sure why she refused to bring her eyes to his.

"Why did you bring my sister to the embassy? That was uncharacteristically kind of you."

The plane cabin was quiet. They were alone inside this section of it, but she knew there were guards beyond the closed doors of where they sat now.

"I know you think me a monster, Reigna. The truth is, when I need to be, I am. But I'm not unnecessarily cruel either. I'm taking you away from your entire life for the next two years. The least I could do is have your closest family member there before I take you."

A knock on the door prevented her from saying anything else. Not that she had anything to say. She was too busy mulling over his words to want to speak any of her own. Had Jasiri ever been cruel to her? No. But the moment she'd rejected him, he'd shut down on her so quickly she'd had a hard time believing anyone who could freeze her out so completely had ever cared for her in the first place.

But this…this was an act of care. Even if he didn't want to acknowledge it and even if she didn't want to believe it. She just didn't know what to do with that.

"Sir," Sherard nodded before stepping into the room and standing next to Jasiri's seat. "We will land in ten minutes. Might we prepare Mrs. Adebesi for what she should expect?"

Reigna stiffened at the sound of that name. She knew Sherard was referring to her, but it felt so strange and disconnected from her, it forced her to draw her eyes across the table to watch the two men.

There was something silent happening between them. Sherard's expression was expectant, and Jasiri's was cold and unyielding.

Sherard cleared his throat before saying, "Fine, sir. I'll leave it to you."

She waited for Sherard to leave before she locked gazes with Jasiri.

"What was all that about? What do I need to be prepared for?"

"My position on Nyeusi is a lot more complicated than you know, and I need to bring you up to speed on some pertinent details you need to be aware of before we step off the plane and encounter what waits for us."

"If you mean your constant entourage, Jasiri, I figured it would probably be bigger in your own country."

"More than you can imagine."

She crossed one leg over the other and grabbed both armrests. It was something her sister called her *bad news posture*. Whenever one of her executives had something bad to tell her, she adopted this pose to maintain her calm and keep the WTF resting on the tip of her tongue from leaping out into the air.

"Jasiri, what's that supposed to mean?"

"It means that when we get off this plane, I need you to follow my lead. You are the wife of a very visible man. From the moment we touch down, all eyes will be on you. Just smile, stay close to me, and look like you're thrilled to be in my country. If you do this for me, I promise to explain everything to you the moment we are inside my private quarters."

She tensed. Her spidey sense was tingling something terrible.

"I come from a billionaire family. I've been around wealth and fame before, Jasiri. Don't worry, I know how to act right in bougie circles. I won't embarrass you."

His face was drawn straight as he looked across the table at her.

"You've been in wealthy circles before, Reigna. But you've never been in royal circles."

She gripped her armrest tighter as she tried to process what he'd said.

"I'm sorry, what did you just say?"

He leaned forward, making sure her gaze was fastened on his before he spoke again.

"Reigna," he spoke her name with quiet strength that let her know he was in control of this conversation. "I am Jasiri Issa Nguvu of the royal house of Adebesi, son of King Omari Jasiri Sahel of the royal house of Adebesi, crown prince and heir apparent to the throne of Nyeusi."

Her jaw dropped as her eyes searched for any hint that he was joking. Unfortunately, the straight set of his jaw and his level gaze didn't say *Girl, you know I'm just playing with you*. Nope, that was a *No lies detected* face staring back at her if she ever saw one.

"You're…you're a…prince?"

"Not *a* prince, *the* prince. As the heir to the throne, I stand above all other princes in the royal line."

She peeled her hand away from the armrest and pointed to herself. "And that makes me…?"

He continued smoothly as if they were having a normal everyday conversation and not one that was literally life-changing. "As my wife, you are now Princess Reigna of the royal house of Adebesi, consort to the heir and future queen of Nyeusi."

Her mind was racing to match the pounding tattoo of her heart. This man, once her lover, now her fake husband, had dropped an unbelievable bomb on her as their plane descended from the sky. And when the wheels hit the tarmac, shaking them in the cabin, four words came out of her mouth.

"Damn. Your. Lying. Ass."

Jasiri watched Reigna as she remained seated in her chair, the picture of calm. He was surprised at just how still and reserved she was. Granted, *Damn. Your. Lying. Ass.* could've been seen as a tad bit aggressive in his circles. But he'd seen Reigna pissed off before, and her response to his admission was pretty tame, considering how he'd thought she'd respond.

Reigna was not a physically violent person. But if you crossed her, she'd cut you into tiny pieces with her tongue, leaving you wondering how someone so beautiful was so lethal that she could make grown men cry.

"You waited until you married me and brought me to your country to tell me you're freakin' royalty? What the absolute hell, Jasiri?"

She unlatched her seat belt with more force than was necessary and stood in the aisle looking down at him. He made the mistake of looking up and meeting the fire flickering in her gaze.

Reigna on any given day was a beautiful woman who could take a man's breath away. Her full curves made him long for the nights he'd had that plush body of hers pressed against him. But the fire in her eyes was indicative of the passion that flamed hot and steady between the two of them. How many times had they argued over something inconsequential that had made desire burn through both like a short fuse to dynamite? Too many to count or too scorching hot to forget.

Watching that familiar flame flash in her eyes made his body tighten in ways and places that he didn't need to entertain at this moment.

She was here to help him save his father and his country. His traitorous body didn't factor into the equation at all.

An ache thrummed through him as if his flesh was saying *Okay, buddy. If you say so.*

Stay focused, Jasiri.

"You are a right SOB, and I knew I shouldn't have trusted your shady ass."

"Reigna," he called, stopping the angry pacing she'd started in the narrow aisle. "We both know if I'd told you before we left America, you would've never agreed to come with me."

"You're damn right," she replied through gritted teeth.

He stood up, blocking her path, making her stand still before him. "My father's health is at stake, and an entire nation rests in the balance. My ascension is about more than me and you.

I had to do whatever was necessary to make sure you accepted this deal."

She titled her head, her eyes wide in disbelief as she just stared at him.

"You say that like it excuses this humongous lie. You've been lying to me since you've known me. Your father hasn't been sick all this time, Jasiri. You've been lying to me since day one."

There it was. The real reason for her anger. Oh, he was not the least bit disillusioned in thinking she was mad about finding out his true identity in this moment. This was about their past and all they'd been to each other.

There, in the depths of her angry eyes he could see the sliver of hurt all that fury covered up. He could see it. It called to the soft spot he had for her that he'd buried beneath all the anger and pain of her rejection. It begged to be set free to comfort her.

He closed his eyes, pinching his brow as he actively worked to get a grip on himself. Reigna was not his priority. His father and his country were. That was all he could focus on. All he would allow himself to focus on.

"There are more important things in the world than your feelings of betrayal, Reigna. As the future, albeit temporary, queen of this nation, you'd better learn that the crown comes before everything and everyone."

A tap at the door followed by Sherard stepping into the room stopped all conversation.

"Your Highness." Sherard's greeting made cold coil in Jasiri's chest. It was a reminder that there was no such thing as privacy when you were a royal, something else he was going to have to explain to Reigna. Outbursts where you could be overheard by staff was a hard and fast no.

Sherard and everyone else in Jasiri's service had been forbidden from using any of his royal titles or styles of address when in Reigna's presence. *Sir* had been the only honorific he'd allowed. Sherard's reference to His Royal Highness meant he'd heard every word of the conversation he and Reigna had just had.

"The king requests an audience with you and the princess," Sherard continued. "We should leave at once if you don't want to keep His Majesty waiting."

"We wouldn't dream of it," Jasiri ground out, knowing his longtime adjutant could read the annoyance in his voice. He turned to Reigna, watching the simmer of concealed anger thrum through her tightly held stance that told him she was using every bit of strength she had to bite her tongue in the moment.

Jasiri extended a hand to her, letting it hang in the air as they engaged in a silent battle with nothing but their gazes before she finally took his offered hand.

"Come, Princess. Our king awaits."

CHAPTER SIX

REIGNA LEANED HER head back against the head-rest of the seat. Jasiri sat next to her in the limo, and as always, his faithful adjutant sat to their side reading off an itinerary to Jasiri.

Reigna was mad.

She was beyond mad.

She was stewing in a boiling pot of pisstivity that she wanted to pour over one Crown Prince Jasiri. But she figured threatening death to the almost sovereign of a nation was probably bad form, so she sat back with her eyes closed try-ing to remember the words to "Children Go Where I Send Thee."

It was an African American spiritual whose upbeat cadence and group participation meant fun times for noisy kids. Ace used to get her and her cousins to sing it when they were get-ting too rowdy around the house. It also re-quired you paid attention to keep all the lyrics in the correct order, so it kept their sugar-fueled brains focused for a short time.

Of all her cousins, she was a pro at this. Could sing all the lyrics in the correct order from one to twelve. But she was so damn mad with Jasiri's I'm-secret-royalty BS and how he'd lied to get her here that she couldn't remember who was born in Bethlehem: Paul, Silas, or the little bitty baby.

"Your Highness," she heard Sherard's voice break through her mental notation of mixed-up Negro Spiritual lyrics in her head. "Is the princess, okay?"

She didn't respond even though a sour *What do you think?* was springboarding off the tip of her tongue.

"It's a lot to take in, Sherard. But she'll be fine."

She'll be fine as soon as she gets you behind closed doors and can wring your royal neck.

The car stopped, and she heard the door open and Sherard shuffle outside of the car before the door closed again.

"Are you going to stay in here and sulk?"

"Sulking is the least destructive thing I could do right now. You might want to leave me to it. Wouldn't want your new wife to cause a royal scandal."

She kept her eyes closed, but she could hear

the small chuckle Jasiri let slide into the air. A memory of the full robust laughter he'd gifted her with when they were curled up inside her apartment or in one of the many hotel rooms around the world they'd shared made her rigid muscles want to relax and melt into the supple car cushions.

"Reigna, I've already told you what's at stake here. I need you to play the role of a woman in love with her prince. We have to sell this if I'm to get the backing of my father's ministry council."

"How long are you gonna use that fate-of-the-country spiel as an excuse for being an ass-hole?"

He chuckled again before letting his thick thigh gently touch hers.

"Reigna, I think we both know I was an ass-hole long before this accession thing became an issue."

He was not wrong.

Jasiri walked into a room knowing who he was. He knew it now as he sat next to her sucking up all the air with his polished sexiness that made you admire and hate him all at the same time. He'd known it then when he'd burrowed himself under her skin in less time than it took to drink a hot cup of a Brooklyn bodega's coffee.

Reigna's mind traveled back to the first time she'd laid eyes on him. He was sitting in Ace's office at Devereaux Inc., laughing with her great-uncle about something too innocuous to remember now. But what she recalled with perfect clarity was the moment he'd stood and greeted her. He was tall, broadly built, with rich dark skin that made her fingers twitch as she fought the urge to reach out and stroke it.

Jasiri had taken one look at her, given her his assured, cocky smile, and they'd both known he had her soul and he'd have her body shortly thereafter.

He'd asked her to walk him to the exit when he was finished meeting with Ace, and before he'd stepped onto the street he'd said, *"You and I are going to enjoy our time together."*

"Our time together?" She'd looked back toward the way they'd come. *"As far as I know, our time together began and ended in the five minutes it took to walk from Ace's office to the front door of this building."*

He'd pushed his hands in his pockets, hitching the corner of his mouth into a wry smile.

"Fierce and unafraid to speak your mind. I like it."

She'd shrugged, placing her hands on her hips to give him her I-am-not-to-be-played-with glare.

*"Not really concerned with whether you like
my attitude or not. I don't know you, and after
five minutes in your presence, I don't really see
a reason to get to know you."*

He'd stroked his chin and glanced up into
the sky, as if he'd needed to draw his answers
from it. But they both knew it was a ruse. Everything about Jasiri, even then, had spoken of
the certainty he had in himself.

"Here's the only reason you need."

He had stepped closer to her, taking her hand
into his and holding it as if she was delicate and
fragile, something to be treasured.

*"A self-possessed woman like you needs a
man with a purpose. A man who understands
his place and power in the world. Anyone else
you'll walk like a dog on a leash, and that kind
of subservience will never satisfy someone
like you who's always seeking to conquer new
things, new people, and the world."*

His arrogance had rolled off him in waves.
That should've been the clue she'd needed to
run far, far away. But instead of running, her
natural competitiveness and her uncontrollable
need to check anyone who crossed her had got
the better of her, and even though his asshole-
ish ways shone through, she'd found herself in
his company and in his bed only a handful of
days later.

The worst of it was the pretty jackass knew the power he wielded, and he made no bones about using it to his advantage. That's exactly what was happening now.

She knew exactly what he was doing. It was obvious. He was trying to get on her good side to get her to do what he wanted. He wasn't even trying to hide how obvious he was being. Except somehow, she could feel the armor of her anger chink just a little, and her laughter tried to squeeze through the weakness in the wall she was trying to build between them.

"Yes," she finally agreed, opening one eyelid to peer up at him. "You are an asshole."

"See?" He shifted in his seat, turning his big body so he fully faced her and that bright and dazzling smile of his beamed down on her like a celestial glow. "We're getting along so much better already."

Nope. She was not letting him charm his way out of this. Not with how he'd played her.

"I don't like being jerked around, Jasiri. Manipulating me into agreeing to marry you when you knew what was waiting for me here was a foul move. I don't know anything about being a royal, let alone the spouse of a monarch. If us pulling this off is as important as you say, how could you think this was a good idea?"

He was quiet long enough that she opened

her other eye to get the full view of him. He was still there, still wearing the dark, tailored suit that he'd worn that morning at their wedding. The arresting way it hugged his muscles made him a captivating figure then. Seated here in the dark cabin of a limousine, he was no less commanding, no less…desirable.

"Reigna, you may not be royal by blood, but you're the most regal woman I know. My mother will teach you how to be a queen. Nevertheless, the style and grace you possess can't be taught. It's something you're born with. I've always known that about you."

She swallowed. Her throat dry and tight, making the forming of simple words impossible as she stared back at this man whose body and personality took up so much space next to her that she was beginning to feel claustrophobic.

This was the *real* Jasiri, crown prince of a nation.

How had she missed it?

Looking at him now, it made so much sense. His natural assurance, the way he always knew he was in control of a room and his surroundings, she'd thought it was just his success as a diplomat that made him so confident. Now, she realized it wasn't everyday confidence. No, he was majestic. He'd been raised since birth to wield his power. Now it was innate, just as natural to him as breathing.

Get a grip, woman. He's the enemy now, remember?

"You really think your mother can teach me to be a queen?"

She expected his smile to broaden, for him to toss some offhanded joke about her lack of preparedness for this wild journey he was about to take her on. His eyes pinned her against the cushions and kept her total focus on him.

"She taught my father to be a king," he answered. His voice was filled with reverence for both his parents, and it warmed her to think of what kind of parents they must've been to engender this type of loyalty and adoration from their son. In just the way he spoke of them, she knew they'd had to be in another league of parenting than her own. "From the way I've watched you run Gemini Queens, you're ten times the leader he was when he first sat on the throne. I think she'll have a much better time with you as her student."

The silence that filled the car was thick and heavy with anticipation as he waited to see if she'd bolt, and she waited to see if he was going to push her past her breaking point. This was part of who they were, who they always had been when they were together. This edging thing where they pushed until the other grew beyond their own expectations, their own capabilities had been both bliss and heartache. Now, here they were again, doing the same.

Before, he'd pushed her until she felt backed into a corner like a wild animal and her only recourse was to come out swinging. She pulled her gaze away from him and looked out at the sprawling castle that sat atop a hill providing the perfect view of the rest of the nation. She closed her eyes, taking a slow deep breath. What would happen now if they pushed each other beyond their breaking point again? There was so much more at stake today than their broken hearts. If they couldn't figure this out, a man's health and a nation's sovereignty hung in the balance.

"Is your faith in your mother's king-making abilities just the overblown adoration of a son, or do you really think she can get me up to speed so we can fool whoever we need to fool?"

His eyes sparked with the same mirth she'd seen when they'd traded barb for barb in one of their teasing sessions of old.

"Oh, I adore my mother. As the former general of the King's Guard, I have a healthy dose of fear where she's concerned too. I've seen that woman cut a hardened military man down with the slant of her eye. Respect her power and be open to listening, and I have no doubt she'll make you the greatest queen Nyeusi has ever seen."

His hard and sharp gaze narrowed on her. It should've made her uncomfortable the way he was looking at her. He wasn't just seeing her, he was seeing through to her, to the possibility of her greatness. And damn if that wasn't just about the sexiest thing she'd ever seen in a man's eye, his absolute belief that she could be and do anything she set her mind to.

It was intoxicating the amount of belief he had in her. It was also terrifying. His firm and unwavering confidence that she could accomplish anything had been one of the most alluring things about Jasiri. It had assured her falling for him more than his charm and good looks had. That thought made a quiver of concern spread through her.

Never again, Reigna. Don't let him lure you down a path you know can only lead to heartache. You know what love gone bad looks like between your parents and between you and Jasiri.

"Ultimately," he continued, drawing her out of her thoughts. "There's one other reason she'll do her best to make sure you can handle your role."

She narrowed her gaze, giving him the unspoken *What's that?* he was waiting for to continue.

"From a mother's perspective, you're the woman who adores her only son. For that, Aziza, daughter of Nuru, would trade her weight in gold to make sure you had all that you needed to fulfill your duties as consort to the new king."

She understood what he was saying. His parents or, at the very least, his mother didn't know this marriage was fake. She also read the underlying subtext that she could never enlighten them about the truth of their nuptials either.

"Trust me, Reigna." His easy smile returned, breaking up the tension in the small space and making it easier for her to relax for a bit. "You are far beyond any expectation that my mother could have for a daughter-in-law. You are your own woman separate from me, and from everything I know about you, you won't give a damn about life at court. To my mother, a hard-nosed military person, that personality quirk will go a long way in gaining her favor."

Reigna quelled the doubt gathering behind her closed lips. If Jasiri's mother was as astute and perceptive as he said, the woman would no doubt pick up on Reigna's distrust of Aziza's son. Because no matter how nice Jasiri appeared in this moment, he was still the man who had walked away from her without a word, never giving her a chance to explain why she'd turned down his proposal. He was also the man who had said and done anything he had to in order to get Reigna exactly where she was. Reigna wasn't sure if she was a good enough actress to make it seem like none of those things mattered.

They mattered a lot.

Grasping at the idea, she grabbed her purse sitting beside her to signal she was ready to step into her new role, no matter how ill-prepared she felt for it. It wouldn't be the first time she owned a role that hadn't been created for her. Gemini Queens Cosmetics thrived because of her leadership and the ingenuity of her brilliant sister. Like Jasiri had said, this was just a different arena.

"You can do this, Reigna," he promised as he tapped on the door alerting the driver standing at the ready to open it.

"I'll hold you to that, Your Highness."

CHAPTER SEVEN

"GOOD GOD ALMIGHTY."

Reigna tried very hard not to act like she'd never been anywhere or seen anything, but the truth was, nothing she'd encountered in her billionaire world measured up to the grandness of Adebesi Palace.

The outside was made of white sandstone that easily blended in with the cool and vibrant tones of an island. Purple domes accented with gold topped the various towers that sprang up like the points of a crown.

She stepped inside what looked like a four-story building fashioned with the largest of the towers on top to see nothing but granite and wood covering the walls, surfaces, and flooring. All the home training that had been grilled into her about how to act in sophisticated places left her, and she had the urge to run her hand over the interior's surfaces while saying *Ooh, this is ni-i-i-ce* in her Tiffany Haddish voice.

"This is your house? You grew up here?"

She glanced at him, unsure what she was expecting to see in his eyes. He stopped to circle just as she did before meeting her gaze.

"This was our main home. We have several smaller ones throughout the island. But this is the one where most state business is conducted. All our governmental buildings are nearby so that the crown can reach all branches of his government quickly, and they him."

She fastened her eyes on the large central stairway with ornate carvings on the wooden banisters that seemed to be trimmed in gold.

"Did you appreciate how amazing this place is as a kid? Or did you slide your disrespectful behind down those gold-trimmed banisters?"

His face lit up as if he was remembering the very thing she'd accused him of.

"I'm afraid I wasn't as appreciative of nice things back then as I am now. As a kid, those banisters were a source of never-ending fun. Today, I recognize them for the gifts from our people that they are. We reside here and can live this way only because we serve the people."

"A lesson that took way too long to take root, if you ask me."

From a side doorway, Reigna saw the woman she recognized through several FaceTime calls Jasiri had included her on to meet his parents. Mrs. Adebesi, as she'd known her then, and Queen Aziza, as she knew her to be now, seemed to float across the room on grace and Black girl magic, and everything in Reigna just wanted to naturally bow to the regal beauty greeting them with a smile.

"My Queen," Jasiri said as he met her in the middle of the foyer, taking her offered hands and kissing the tops of them. "It's so good to see you again."

She shook her head and then wagged her finger at him as if chastising him.

"I am Mama," she said matter-of-factly and then glanced over quickly to Reigna. "As of today, she is your queen. Understood?"

This woman wasn't even talking to her, and Reigna was ready to nod right along with Jasiri, agreeing to everything his mother had just said.

She stepped away from her son and headed toward Reigna, and suddenly Reigna felt awkward and uncomfortable. Was she supposed to bow, curtsy, kneel? She had no idea.

This regal woman, who looked to be about the same just over five feet height that Reigna possessed, with her deep curves draped in a form-fitting purple peplum skirt suit and a matching Gele head wrap, that told anyone who laid eyes on her that she ran things, captivated Reigna, freezing her where she stood.

"I'm not sure how to properly greet you. I've never met a queen before," Reigna admitted, not wanting Queen Aziza to think ill of her simply because she was ignorant of their ways.

Aziza's warm brown skin glowed as her mouth spread into a wide grin. "A simple *Hello, Mama* and a hug will suffice."

Not waiting for Reigna to respond, the woman grabbed her up in a hearty hug, one where you had to sway back and forth to keep from toppling over. It was warm and inviting, and even though she'd only known the queen for two minutes, Reigna's body melted into hers like she was starved for matronly affection.

Queen Aziza pulled back sooner than Reigna would've liked. That warmth had felt glorious as it spread from the core of her chest out to her limbs.

"Now, let me take a look at you. You are absolutely gorgeous, daughter."

Reigna blinked at the word, wondering if she'd misheard the woman.

"You are mine, as much as that bullheaded son of mine is."

Reigna glanced over to see Jasiri give his mother a playful eye roll. The way she smiled in response it was obvious she knew her son meant no disrespect.

"Know from this moment on, my darling, it

is as if you were born to me too. There are no such things as in-laws here on Nyeusi. Considering how our nation was formed, kinship played a huge role in our enslaved ancestors escaping and building a new world upon this land. Family, whether born or chosen, functioned the same for them and now for us. That means I am your mother now, Reigna, and the king is now your father. That is the Nyeusi way."

Reigna could feel heat suffuse her brown skin, and she had to stop herself from swiping at her eyes or she knew the tears would come.

Never in all her thirty-four years had any woman, even her mother and grandmothers, ever made her feel this loved and cared for the way a child seeks to be nurtured by a mother figure.

Reigna's mother had seen her twin daughters as nothing but a nuisance. She'd snap at them whenever they made too much noise, whenever they'd asked her to play with them. Hell, them breathing too loudly was enough to garner her wrath. Reigna had always ached to leave school and have her mother scoop her up into a big hug like she'd seen her classmates' mothers do. All she'd gotten was an employed driver holding a door open for her and silence when she'd walked into their family home.

Ignoring the ache her mother's absence had

caused had become a usual part of Reigna's existence. Ignoring the neglect had meant rarely taking the time to think about how much she lacked for as a girl. Unfortunately, after experiencing just one hug from Aziza, Reigna was painfully aware of how much she'd been denied as a child.

Thank goodness Ace had been everything to his twin great-nieces. Due to his love, it had never occurred to her, and Reigna was pretty sure she could speak for Regina on this point too, that not having a mother figure had meant they'd missed out on something.

But standing in the warmth of this great and powerful woman, Reigna could suddenly feel the emptiness that this woman was actively filling. This role that Reigna was going to actively let her fill even though she knew it was only going to be temporary.

Again, there was no rule saying this entire experience had to be miserable for her and Jasiri and, by extension, his parents. They each could take what they needed. If Aziza wanted a daughter, Reigna would happily accept her as a mother, because in this moment where she was out of her depth, Reigna realized she needed and wanted one more than anything.

"Thank you, Mama" was all she could manage without bursting into a blubbering bag of water. It was also all she could manage to get past the hardening ball of guilt lodging itself firmly in her throat.

Reigna was wrong for this. She knew that as well as she knew her name, all while intentionally ignoring that knowledge. What did it say about her that after experiencing Aziza's genuine affection, Reigna didn't want to be right?

Aziza must have divined Reigna was about to break against her emotional wall because she straightened her shoulders and said, "Now that we've gotten that straight," she took Reigna's hand into her own, "let's go meet the king."

Jasiri walked behind the queen and Reigna, a tight knot balled up in the middle of his chest as he recounted the brief exchange between his mother and his wife. Never having had any kind of real relationship with her own mother, he could see the relief that bled through Reigna's body when his mother had taken her into her arms.

He knew how serious his mother was about their family. He should've never allowed her to get so close to Reigna so quickly, especially since he knew their marriage was on borrowed time. But knowing how Reigna's toxic relationship with her parents had warped her sense of connection, he couldn't take the warmth his mother provided away from his bride.

He shouldn't care. This would only last for two years. But he wanted it for her. Since his mother had given him the excuse to go along with it because it was what the soon-to-be queen mother wanted, he could let it happen and ignore the guilt his dishonestly spun inside him. He could also ignore the extra thump in his chest when he saw his mother fawning over his wife.

This is what they would've had two years ago if Reigna hadn't rejected him. The only difference was that then he could've had the total package. A mother who adored him and the woman he loved. Now he'd just have to settle for his mother adoring Reigna. That would just have to be good enough because that was all there could ever be.

He would never allow a woman, especially Reigna, the power to hurt him, to control his heart, and therefore him ever again. Not even for the happiness of his beloved mother.

His mother opened the double doors to the king's office, and there he found his father sitting behind his desk, looking not as strong as Jasiri would like him to be, but he was in command of himself, the frailty of his hospital bed left behind.

The king stood, walking in front of the desk,

and Jasiri knelt on one knee, taking his father's right hand into his and kissing the royal ring of a golden lion's head with purple sapphire eyes to signify his leadership and his royal status.

His mother wore a matching one with a lioness's head, and the same royal purple eyes that embodied her position as the consort to the Great Lion of Nyeusi.

He brought his forehead closer to his father's ring, letting the cool metal touch his skin.

Jasiri had always known this ring would be his one day as the heir apparent. But never had he imagined it would come so soon. He pushed down the sadness thoughts of his father's health brought to his heart and instead focused on the blessing in this moment. Thrones usually passed from father to son in death. Yet his father was still here, reminding Jasiri the upheaval to his life was a small sacrifice to pay to see his father alive and healthy again.

"My King," he uttered as he stood. "I am glad to see you looking better. But don't you think you should stay away from this desk?"

"Do you see this, Aziza? He gets married and thinks he's king already. Where is my new daughter you've brought me? Let me focus on her instead of your fussing."

Jasiri stepped aside so his father could see Reigna standing next to his mother. She looked less uncomfortable than she had upon meeting his mother, and Jasiri knew he was right in asking his mother to take on Reigna's royal training. Any staff member could've taken that on, but his mother would teach Reigna while building her confidence in navigating this new world Jasiri had brought her into.

She needed the confidence of a queen. Otherwise, this would never work. The council would never approve his accession, and if he took the throne without their blessing, it would leave room for his uncle to try to lay claim to the throne.

That could never stand.

"Come, daughter." The king waved his hand, bidding Reigna to step toward him. When she stood before him, he clasped her hands into his. "You are even more beautiful in person than you were on the few video calls we shared."

The king returned his attention to Jasiri. "I knew then from those short chats that you'd chosen well in a partner. I'm glad to see that you fixed whatever was wrong between the two of you, Jasiri. The wisest decision a king can make is who he chooses to be at his side."

Jasiri watched as his father returned his gaze back to Reigna, squeezing her hands in his. "Forgive us for not revealing to you who Jasiri was. We have always agreed to support him in however he chose to show up into the world.

It made us proud that he wanted you to know him as a man and not a prince. It meant that he really wanted you to love him. My only regret was that keeping that knowledge from you resulted in you walking away from what the two of you shared."

He saw the flash of questions in Reigna's eyes, and he simply nodded. Yes, he'd told his parents that she felt betrayed by him keeping his royal secret because it was the only thing that let both him and Reigna off the hook with respect to blame. She'd angered him to the point that he was hardly able to comport himself and be the charming prince his birthright had demanded he be. But he'd never, never wanted his parents to think ill of her.

She spoke to the king but kept her eyes on Jasiri. "I'm sorry I reacted so poorly. I only hope I can show you I'm made of stronger stuff than my response may have led you to believe."

Was she saying those words for his parents' benefit or his?

Jasiri closed his eyes, trying to keep himself from reading more into this than there was. The truth was, it didn't matter if she was sincere. She'd shown him who she really was when she'd rejected him. She hadn't wanted him then, and he'd never give her a second chance to have him now.

CHAPTER EIGHT

AFTER MEETING WITH his parents, the two of them walked to what Jasiri explained were his apartments, or his wing of the palace.

They were standing in the middle of what looked like a living room but on an elevated scale, with warm shades of brown, burgundy, and beige creating an inviting feel that almost made you forget the vaulted ceilings or the priceless artwork with African heritage sprinkled throughout.

A long quiet stretched between them, and Reigna wasn't quite sure how to deal with it. Something had happened in that brief exchange between them in his father's office, and she didn't know how to handle it.

The smart thing would've been to ignore it and pretend it didn't happen. But Reigna didn't build the business she had by ignoring things. She envisioned something she wanted, and she went for it. Yet that tactic didn't seem quite right when it came to Jasiri. Partly because she was nowhere near ready to admit that she wanted anything from him but his half of Ace's house.

This was an emotionally taxing day. She'd been overwhelmed by so many different feelings that she couldn't swear in a court of law exactly what she wanted. At least that's what her brain was saying. She figured it was a safer option to follow it instead of her heart. Especially when being in the presence of Jasiri's family was doing strange things to it.

"This is our quarters. Our bedroom is through that door to the back right, the kitchen and dining areas are through the front left, and the balcony is through the back left."

He pointed back toward the front door that they'd entered.

"The more formal rooms for gathering, cooking, state affairs, and the library are all on the first floor. The private gardens are in the back, along with a personal gym and a swimming pool. Just ask me or any of the staff to show you how to get to whatever until you learn your way around the palace."

She blinked rapidly at him. She'd heard all he'd said, but her brain kept circling back to one thing.

"I'm sorry," she said and held up a finger.

"Did you say *our bedroom*, as in we'll be sharing one?"

"Of course I did."

He loosened the knot of his tie, then removed his jacket before beckoning her to follow him. She'd hoped to find a large room with two beds that would make this *our bedroom* thing make sense. But nope, that's not at all what she found.

A four-poster elevated king-size bed with linen drapes from the overhead canopy tied to each post.

"There have got to be other bedrooms in this palace for me to sleep in."

"Of course there are," he replied. His matter-of-factness grated on her nerves just a little bit.

"Jasiri, this is a fake marriage. What happened to 'I've never had a woman in my bed who didn't want to be there'?"

"That's true. That will always be true," he countered. He sat down on the foot bench in front of the bed, laying his jacket and tie on one side of him while he patted the empty space on the other.

She complied, figuring blowing up probably wouldn't resolve this issue in any way that was conducive to them keeping this fragile peace they seemed to be attempting since she'd met his parents.

"Reigna, there is no such thing as privacy

when you're a member of the royal family. If anyone discovers the true nature of our union, all will be lost. If you and I sleep in separate rooms, the staff will talk. We can't have that getting out."

She ran her fingers through her long braids, trying to make sense of what Jasiri was saying to her.

"I thought all you royal types slept in separate beds all the time, like it was some sort of rule."

He shook his head. "Americans really need to stop using *The Crown* for their only understanding of royal life."

She chuckled because that was exactly where she'd gotten that information from.

"The Adebesis are not any other royal family. It may be customary in some royal homes for couples to sleep in separate rooms, but that's not how it works on Nyeusi. The monarch and his consort are a team, they always present a united front, and they work as one in all things. You must sleep here with me."

Her deep breath seemed to echo off the high ceiling and the walls of the large room.

"Jasiri, you're a cuddler. This isn't going to work."

"No," he corrected, "I was a cuddler with

you. But if you want me to keep my hands to myself, I promise that won't be a problem."

She stood up, pacing a bit to get her thoughts together. Did she think it was a great idea tempting fate by them sleeping in the same bed? No. But they were adults, and she was certain they could make this work.

"You said the monarch and his consort always present a united front. Is that true?"

He simply nodded in response.

"If we're going to do the same, we have to work on you being honest with me, Jasiri."

"Reigna," he said and sighed, "I've already told you why I kept you in the dark."

She held up a hand to stop him. "We're past all that, Jasiri. While I still don't agree with how you kept me in the dark throughout or relationship and you negotiating with me in bad faith, I understand why you did what you did. What I want to know is that from now on, you're going to keep me in the loop from start to finish."

The pinched furrow of his brow told her he was seriously contemplating her words. Good. If this was going to work, he had to consider her.

"Jasiri, I won't be ambushed like this ever again. If you want me to be your partner, present this united front you keep talking about, then I expect to be treated as your partner. And as such, I have a couple of demands I'm going to add to our agreement."

He quirked a brow. "But our agreement has already been made."

"Nope," she replied with an over exaggerated shake of her head. "You're not going to sit here and pretend like contracts aren't addended or outright renegotiated all the time, especially when one party negotiates in bad faith."

She had him, and the reluctant way he narrowed his gaze was confirmation of that.

"Fine. What are your new terms?"

"I want to be the last one in the room with you when you make your decisions. You can't expect me to play my role if I'm kept in the dark. You want me to stay here? To help you stabilize your nation? Then, you do me the courtesy of keeping me aware of everything that's going on. Otherwise," she said and pointed to the window, "I'll be on the first thing smoking out of here and leave you to your own devices."

She meant every word she'd said. Yes, she'd lose Ace's house, but in the moment, somehow, she knew this was a stance she had to take. Reigna didn't do fake. She was either all in or she couldn't be bothered in the first place. Everything she'd witnessed since she'd landed on this island told her this venture with Jasiri would be no different from the ones she conducted in the boardroom. They were either going to work together or not at all.

She watched his dark brown eyes spark with something like interest. Amusement? Pride? Or maybe some combination of all three. Jasiri had always played his cards close to the vest, and she figured the incongruous look on his face was probably his usual when it came to contract negations.

"You really want to be my queen in the truest sense?"

She sighed deeply, pausing a moment before she replied. "I don't think there's any way around it if the scrutiny you've said we'll be under is accurate."

He stood, extending his hand as he said, "I hope you understand what you're getting yourself into. I trust you to know your own mind, however. If you want to be my business partner in this venture, then that's exactly what you'll be."

When she accepted his hand and gave it a hardy shake, she attempted to take it back and he held on to it tighter before looking deeply into her eyes saying, "Long live Queen Reigna of the House of Adebesi. Long live the queen."

* * *

Jasiri stood in the gardens replaying the conversation he'd had with Reigna about being partners. This was the best-case scenario he could've hoped for. Reigna bringing her considerable leadership skills to help him settle into his role as king. Then, why did he feel trouble looming just beyond the horizon as he considered what working this closely to Reigna could really mean?

He wanted off this mental roller-coaster, where he couldn't figure out whether to draw near or run for the nearest exit where Reigna was concerned. No matter how much he wanted to accept her generous offer of partnership, in his head, *What happens when she leaves?* played over on a never-ending loop that he couldn't see how to break free from.

Two years. She'd be leaving in two years. That was their agreement. Getting attached would only bring trouble to his feet that neither he nor his people needed. A distracted king was a bad king, and after all he'd sacrificed to ascend to the office, he wasn't going to do his people the disservice of letting himself lose focus on what was important.

Running from the distraction of her was how he'd ended up standing right where he was in the garden. He'd managed to keep things compartmentalized until he'd walked into their bedroom to grab the laptop he'd left on the nightstand when he'd found her asleep, curled up on one side over the duvet in the large bed looking like she belonged there all along.

This was what he'd wanted when he proposed to her. He'd wanted stolen moments like this where he could forget his title and lose himself in the woman he loved.

How did that work out for you?

His cruel memory letting him grasp his hope in one moment while rubbing the truth of his failed past with this woman in his face in the next was nasty work. It was unnecessarily cruel, while warning him away from danger at the same time to make sure he learned his lesson.

"This is not about what you shared, Jasiri." He whispered those words so low he barely heard them himself. "It's about your father and Nyeusi. Nothing more. Nothing less."

He needed to put distance between himself and Reigna and the conflicting thoughts he was having about her. Jasiri left his apartments, walking toward the steps that would lead to the administrative wing of the palace when he heard a loud voice coming from his father's office.

He quickly headed in the direction of the

noise, tensing when he saw his father's guards standing at the door poised, ready to move in at the hint of their king's bidding.

"Your Highness," they greeted Jasiri but kept their entire focus on the door.

"What's happening in there?"

"Prince Pili demanded to speak with the king. We tried to keep him away, but the king insisted he'd speak with him."

Understanding dawned. Only one thing could make Pili this angry, and Jasiri was certain it had nothing to do with the king's health.

"Contact the guards in my wing, and have someone bring the princess here to me. When she arrives, let her walk directly in."

If Reigna wanted to be his partner, showtime was about to start now.

He moved beyond the guards and stepped into his father's office seeing his parents sitting on a high-backed sofa together while his uncle paced back and forth.

"I cannot believe you would allow the prince to do something so dishonest. Anyone with eyes can see he only married this American to be able to ascend to the throne. As beloved as your son is, Omari, he is not ready to rule our great nation."

"I'm not?" Jasiri asked, his words stopping Pili's motion dead in his tracks. "Baba, I guess all those civics and comportment classes I've endured over the years have been a waste."

"Nephew," Pili growled, "show some respect for your elders. This is not a joking matter."

Oh, did this man annoy the hell out of Jasiri. He always had. He stood more than a head shorter than Jasiri's six feet two inches. Where Jasiri and his father walked with confidence and treated their countrymen with care, Pili walked through life thinking his royal blood made him special and everyone should bow to him. Unlucky for him, Jasiri had never bought into Pili's self-indulgent script. Even worse, Jasiri's father had taught him that a man was only as good as he treated the least of those around them. By that measure, Pili was the worst example of a man and a king that there could be.

"The only joke in this room is you coming here pretending to care about anything other than your place in the line of succession."

Pili snatched his gaze away from Jasiri and took an angry step toward the king. Jasiri watched closely as his mother crossed her leg and rested one of her hands beneath the crossed leg.

He knew for a fact that as the former general of the King's Guard, she was never without a weapon or a means to defend herself or those she loved.

As if on cue, his mother said, "Make that the last step you take toward your king, Pili. I wouldn't want to see you hurt." Pili instantly stepped back, to Jasiri's relief. He wasn't worried in the slightest for his mother's or father's safety. Hell, he wasn't even worried for his own. It was mandatory that senior members of the royal family all mastered self-defensive arts. History had taught them all too well what happened when royals thought they were safe.

Jasiri's only concern about this moment escalating was the blasted paperwork he'd have to fill out as a witness to treason against the crown.

He pinched the bridge of his nose to bring his mind back to focus. He would be king soon. Annoyance or threat, he would have to deal with Pili sooner or later. No need in delaying the future.

"Prince Pili," Jasiri called his name with the authority of a king. He wanted this man to know he wasn't speaking to his nephew, he was speaking to the imminent ruler of Nyeusi. "Your concern has been noted."

"Are you dismissing me?" Pili's face contorted into a twisted frown, as if the idea that Jasiri was exerting authority over him physically pained the man.

"Yes, I am. You've voiced your opinion regarding my ascension. What more is there to say?"

Jasiri was about to walk away until Pili said, "You married an outsider." His words were like sharp rocks against delicate skin. The idea of anyone putting Reigna in a box of any kind made his blood boil.

"You would be wise to mind your words, Prince Pili."

"You heard what I said, Jasiri. You married an outsider. You didn't even have the decency to choose a spouse born of Nyeusian blood. She's one of the Lost Tribe, for God's sake. What were you thinking?"

Jasiri's body tensed, and he had to fight to remember that he was beyond reducing himself to a simple brawl because he wanted to snatch his uncle's disrespectful lips from his face. Before he could restrain his anger enough to be certain his reply would be verbal and not a clenched fist to the jaw, the familiar sound of Reigna's voice filled the room.

"The Lost Tribe?" she questioned with raised brows as she entered. "What exactly does that mean, and how did I end up joining it?"

All eyes focused on Reigna's form. She was dressed in what could only be called as a power suit. The red material pulled over her curves just the right way while the vibrant color and high bun she'd twisted her braids into on the top of her head let everyone know this woman hadn't come to play. If there was any doubt in that, the self-assured way she carried herself in those impossibly high stiletto heels said it all. She never put a step out of place and if you wanted to tussle with her, you'd better come prepared.

CHAPTER NINE

REIGNA DIDN'T NEED to know the specifics to understand what was going on here. The guards had said Prince Pili, the brother of the king, was making a fuss about Jasiri's ascension. From the bit she'd walked in on, he was specifically upset about who Reigna was. Or, more important, what she wasn't: Nyeusian. As a Black woman running a *Fortune 500* company, being unwelcome at the table wasn't foreign to her. As this Prince Pili would soon learn, it didn't scare her either. It just made her more determined to succeed.

Ace had once told her, "If they refuse to make room for you at the table, kick the door open and sit down like you belong there, because you do. Then you stare every one of those cowards in the eye and dare any one of them to try to make you get up."

That was her motto. She owned everything she touched, and this royal thing would be no different as far as she was concerned.

As if she'd done it a thousand times before, she walked into the room and mimicked what she'd seen Jasiri do when greeting his parents. She knelt in front of the monarch and his consort, taking both their right hands in each of hers. She kissed the head of his father's lion ring and said, "My King," then repeated the process for Jasiri's mother and said, "My Queen."

She stood, keeping their hands in hers. "Baba, Mama, please forgive my delay. I guess I was more tired from our travel than I realized. As soon as my head touched the pillow, I dozed off."

Both the king's and queen's smiles silently told her *Give him a show, daughter.*

She felt a familiar weight on her hip and instantly knew Jasiri was touching her. They might have been apart for two years, but when a person touches you with such strength, awareness, and entitlement, you remember it like you remember your own name.

His lips settled on her temple and instinctively she melted into him, placing her hand on his large bicep for purchase. She was playing a role for the benefit of his uncle, keeling over in her stilettos just wouldn't do.

"Did you rest well, my love?"

His voice was so sincere she could almost forget that this was just for show. It felt natural to her ears to hear him use such an endearment to address her, and her body's natural reaction was to calm in the presence of his security.

She closed her eyes briefly, one to revel in the balm of his voice and the comfort of his touch, but also to remind herself that this wasn't real. She had to remember that. Forgetting would cost her a lot more than Ace's house.

"I did rest well. I'm sorry if I delayed any plans you'd set forth." She looked over to where Pili stood with a mix of anger and confusion, as if he couldn't figure out if the scene he was witnessing was real or not.

Good. Confusing your enemy was a good strategy for victory.

"This is my uncle, Prince Pili. His visit was unexpected." Jasiri tightened his hold on Reigna's waist. It could just be part of the ruse they were putting on. Somehow, it didn't feel that way. She was pretty certain it was a protective measure.

In all her years in the corporate world, she'd learned to follow her instincts. So if Jasiri's was telling him to keep her close in the presence of this man, she wouldn't fight him.

"Princess." Pili cleared his throat. "Forgive me. I meant no disrespect."

She raised an eyebrow. The way Pili's eyes

darted from side to side said he'd realized he'd said the quiet part out loud.

"Sure you did, Pili." His features held still. That was the true markings of a politician or a PR person. But he couldn't hide the slight widening of his irises that expressed his shock. "I might not know what the Lost Tribe is, but it's obvious it wasn't meant as an endearment. What I do understand is that you'd prefer Jasiri had married someone who was born on Nyeusi and raised in its culture."

She stepped out of Jasiri's grasp because everyone in that room knew that Pili was now on the ropes. He'd relinquished any standing the moment his elitism had gotten the better of him.

"The problem is that's not who Jasiri chose. I'm not just some random person off the street. I'm someone who your nephew took the time to learn about and love."

She turned slightly to glimpse Jasiri. His face was inscrutable, and she couldn't readily read what was going through his head. Whatever it was, he extended his hand to hers and when she took it, he laced his fingers through hers, anchoring her in the moment and in her place by his side.

"If given the same opportunity," she continued. "I would like to learn about and love Nyeusi's culture and her people as well."

She bowed her head slowly toward the king and queen, hoping she conveyed the sincerity she had in her heart. This marriage and her role may be temporary, but she would do all she could to support this family and this nation for the duration of her time here.

"If that's your only concern about my marriage and Jasiri's ascension, I can promise you that you have nothing to worry about. As his consort, I will always put this nation first, no matter where I originate from or where my bloodline traces back to."

"Princess," Pili tried to interrupt but she ignored him and continued on. It wasn't in her nature to give elitist bullies a moment of grace.

"Pili, as I said, if your concerns about my marriage and Jasiri's ascension rest in fear regarding the preservation of this country's culture and history, you have nothing to worry about. But if your concern rests in the fact that you don't want Jasiri on the throne because you want it for yourself, then you'll come to understand what everyone who underestimates me does. To do so pretty much solidifies your own peril."

Pili flinched as if she'd struck him, and Reigna smiled. She'd thrown down the gauntlet and let Jasiri's enemy know she wasn't to be played with. It was up to him now to decide if he'd heed her warning or not.

She turned to the king and queen and gave a quick bow of her head. "Baba, Mama, if you require nothing further of our presence, the prince and I aren't yet settled into our apartments. Please excuse us."

"Of course." The queen stood, grabbing Reigna into another tight hug. "We know you two must be tired after your journey. Take the night and the day to get settled and meet us for dinner tomorrow in our private quarters at six sharp. We await your arrival."

"Thank you, Mama."

She looked down at her and Jasiri's entwined fingers, realizing he hadn't yet released her. She made no move to disengage them. She liked the feel, the power of them joined together.

"My prince," she said as she purposely softened her features and offered him a welcoming smile. "Shall we?"

He nodded, then gave brief nods to his parents. He led her to the door, stopping to open it. He turned his gaze to his parents once again.

"Baba, Mama, don't overexert yourselves." He narrowed his eyes and gave Pili a hard glare. "Uncle, do not overstay your very limited welcome."

Just like that, Jasiri ended the discussion, and

they walked out of the room. Two things had happened in that encounter. One, she'd made it clear that she was Jasiri's partner, and she wasn't afraid of his uncle. Although her family was wealthy, Reigna had grown up in Brooklyn, and she wasn't unaccustomed to metaphorically scrapping when she needed to. Two, Jasiri had made it clear, he was the next and true ruler of this nation, and if Pili wanted to challenge that, he'd have the fight of his life on his hands.

When they were back in their apartments, Jasiri turned to her and said, "I'd forgotten how fierce you were in a power suit."

She slid her hands down the front of her suit and then the sides of her updo hairstyle.

"I don't play when I'm in my battle armor."

"A note well taken." He took a deep breath before he turned serious eyes to her. "You really meant it when you said you wanted to be my partner in all this, didn't you?"

She tilted her head as she gazed up at him. This wasn't small talk. Jasiri truly wanted to know her answer to his question.

"As I said before, I'm still pissed with the antics you pulled to get me to agree to this, Jasiri. But after meeting your uncle and suffering his bullshit elitism, I'm in ten toes down. There's no version of this where I sit back and do nothing while he tries to steal your throne. If he wants a fight…"

She squared up like she was facing an opponent in a boxing ring.

"Then ring the bell, dammit, and let's go."

CHAPTER TEN

JASIRI STOOD ON the balcony looking out over the ocean view. He'd specifically chosen this part of the palace as his own because of the calming effect the push and pull of the ocean to and from the coast always made him feel whole. It was like the waves were reaching for him, returning each time to come back to him.

Once he'd returned home after Reigna rejected him, part of him had held on to the dream that someday she'd come reaching for him too, the same way the great waters that fed life to his land did.

"Jasiri?"

As if he'd conjured her with his mind, Reigna stood in the sitting room, just beyond the doors to the balcony.

"I didn't mean to disturb you. I thought it might be nice to get some air on the balcony." She pointed her thumb over her shoulder before continuing. "If you want to be alone, I can certainly find somewhere else to be in this ridiculously large space."

"It is rather ridiculous, isn't it?" Having grown up in this space, he spoke those words with honesty.

Her eyes widened as she held out the palm side of her hand.

"I didn't mean to offend you. This place is the most gorgeous thing I've ever seen. I just never imagined anyone living in something that looks like it was magic, hand-painted by God. Considering I grew up in luxury, that's saying something."

"No offense taken." He gestured for her to stand beside him, and he was glad to see she'd come willingly. "Everything is relative. It wasn't until I'd become the Nyeusian ambassador that I realized just how extravagant my life was. It humbled me. Kept me grateful for who I am and grounded about the duties I was born to fulfill."

She studied him for a moment, and he wondered what she was trying to see. She'd already known Jasiri the man. He'd never had the opportunity to show her Jasiri the dutiful prince, though.

That regret, like so many others he buried in his gut trying to forget and disassociate himself from, sat heavy at his core. It weighed him down, kept him tied to it no matter how desperately he wanted to be free.

"Have you eaten, yet? I didn't have the heart to wake you after you went down again once we dealt with Pili in my father's office."

It was an obvious ploy to throw her off his scent. Her pointed gaze and the wry twist of her mouth told him she wasn't fooled by his antics either.

"I found the kitchen and made myself a quick sandwich when I woke up. I guess between the travel, stepping inside a real-life palace, and meeting a king and queen—not to mention the opening scrimmage with your uncle—I couldn't seem to keep my eyes open once I sat down."

She looked out into the ocean, seemingly captivated by the same ebb and flow that had him rooted to this spot himself.

"Speaking of Pili, he's not going to make your ascension easy, is he?"

"Not one bit," he replied making them both chuckle at the inevitable fight they knew awaited them.

"I'm not afraid of him."

Although she continued to gaze at the water, her words gripped him, making him look directly at her profile. She was breathtaking, no matter the angle. Watching the light breeze shift her braids, his fingers itched to touch the end of one. He wanted to twist it back and forth between his fingertips over and over again until his stress bled out of him.

"I know you're not afraid of him, Reigna. That's why I brought you here. I knew you were the one person I could trust to have my back when it came to Pili."

Her brows furrowed and she pursed her lips, silently asking why.

"Two reasons. One, you're the most loyal person I know. Just look at the lengths you went to just to snatch Ace's home from my clutches."

She opened her mouth to speak and then closed it abruptly because they both knew his recollection of the facts was true.

"Two, you don't like bullies. I've seen you cut some of the richest and most powerful people down to size in defense of someone who couldn't defend themselves. I knew you'd never willingly stand by and let Pili corrupt the throne."

Her hands were on her hips, and he could see her searching for an argument where there was none. She glanced up at him, taking a deep breath and then releasing it into the quiet of the night.

"I guess you got me there. I really can't stand that man, and I only spent five minutes in his presence."

"Pili tends to have that effect on people." He moved closer, laying one hand on the stone railing and using his finger to pull her gaze up to his. "Never underestimate him, though. He's sneaky, ruthless, and relentless. Always keep your guard up when it comes to him. I don't want to see anything happen to you, Reigna."

He hoped she could understand what he was really saying. He certainly didn't have the words to express it verbally. The idea of her coming to harm because of Pili burned through him like hot metal on skin. It would mark his soul in a way he wasn't sure he could ever recover from.

"I see it now."

"See what?" His voice was gruff but not as stern as he'd wanted it to be. It seemed whenever he was in this woman's presence he could never get his body to do as he'd directed.

"All the arrogance and obsession with control, I thought it was just your overinflated ego. It was more than that, though? Wasn't it?"

She leaned closer to him, placing her hand atop his on the stone railing of the balcony.

This is not good.

He should've heeded that thought and left right then before her wide, soulful eyes looked up at him. The glint of the moonlight bounced off the ocean and into her pupils, making the brown pools turn to glass. Glass that reflected into the depths of his soul giving a clear view of everything he was trying to hide from her.

"Yes."

The word slipped from his lips like a petal on the breeze, easy, without the ability to steer or control where he'd land. He gripped the stone beneath his hand in an effort not to grip hers. If he returned her touch, it would be his undoing, and then where would he be?

Right back at her feet, rejected at her whim.

"If meeting my uncle today didn't teach you anything else, it should relay how heavy the burden of succession is. My life has been written for me since before I was born."

He tried to stop there, but her pleading gaze silently asked him to continue, and he couldn't help but oblige.

"My name, my occupation, my education, my place in the world, it was all locked in place from the moment my parents learned of my conception. It can easily take control of you if you don't have the skills or the desire to control it."

"Don't you ever get tired of always being in control, hypervigilant, Jasiri? Don't you want to let go sometimes?"

Her hand began to glide up his hand and beyond his wrist. He stood rod straight, apprehensive about where her touch would lead to but still so desperate for it, he refused to push her away. She let her hand move up his arm and over his chest, resting it above the strong thud of his heart before her eyes met his.

"If only for one night," she continued as she stepped into the circle of his arms and pulled them around her. "Don't you just want to let go?"

"Every goddamn second of every day."

His voice was gravel against rough sand, scraping up the tender flesh of his throat as he ground those words out. The closest he'd ever come to it was the moments he'd spent in her arms. Her touch had done more than just excite him: it had healed something broken in him that he'd never been able to name. With her looking at him, no, through him, he could see from her perspective what had been missing before and after her. It was his ability to just be himself.

With Reigna, he didn't have to carry a title or responsibilities. The crown wasn't looming over him like a recurrent bad dream that was just waiting for him to fall deep enough asleep until it hijacked his dreams. As long as he was with her, his title felt like a job he left at the end of the business day. When he crossed Reigna's threshold, he was a real man, not a title. Not a cog in a nearly three-hundred-year-old machine.

"Jasiri?"

She put her hand in his and slowly walked

them to the bathroom. She left him standing in the middle of the large room to turn on the shower heads. Like so many other places in the palace, it was too large and ostentatious to be called by its functional name. Yes, this was technically a bathroom. The multihead shower with the large marble bench long enough that Jasiri at over six feet could lie comfortably on it took up one wall on its own. Its glass enclosure so clear you could hardly tell it was there. This was a spa.

Even if you could ignore the shower, the gold-encrusted basins and the wall and flooring tiles made of onyx and marble made it clear that this room, like every other in the palace, was an experience.

Reigna made quick work of undressing them both. Once she covered her head with a shower turban, she waited until he donned his too, then without preamble she pulled them inside and under the spray.

The moment the water touched his skin all the noise in his head stopped and all he could see was her. Her full, luscious body slick with water, begging for his touch. He'd been taught to control his urges lest they control him. As a king, you could never allow anything or anyone that kind of power over you. Her full lips with the perfect bow opened slightly and said the two words he'd never been able to resist coming from her.

"Jasiri, please."

He heard the brittle snap of his control echo off the glass enclosure and any hopes he had of resisting Reigna were gone. He pulled her to him, consuming her mouth in a greedy kiss as he pressed her back into the cool wall. She'd wanted him to let go, and dear God, he'd give her everything she'd asked for.

"On the bench now, Princess."

Reigna had meant to comfort the man, help him lay down his heavy burdens for just a few moments. How that had landed with her in the supine position on this giant marble bench while Jasiri stalked over her like she was his prey, she didn't know, and she didn't care. The same fire that blazed in his eyes before he wrung both their bodies dry of pleasure flashed in front of her now. This wasn't a warning. It was a promise, and Reigna was here for every pledged moment of it.

Jasiri's hands were all over her, stroking her expectant skin. His mouth found her nipple, licking and grazing it with his teeth until it was taut and stiff. He worried it until she was squirming with need beneath him.

Jasiri's touch had always been the truest

thing she'd known in her life. His touch instantly meant she'd splinter into pleasure, and there had never been a moment when that wasn't true with him.

He loomed above her with his one hand planted just above her head on the marble bench and one of his knees rested against the outer shell of her hip. She felt his other hand slip between her wet folds, caressing her nub until it hummed with a delicious ache. She lifted her hips, chasing his touch, and he rewarded her by applying a light pat against it that made her shudder with her desire for him. Before she could recover, his fingers were inside her, plunging, searching, and scissoring until they found that hidden spot within her core that made her body tighten and her breath catch.

Their eyes met in the haze of the water, steam, and need, and when she lifted her hips again, this time he didn't make her wait. He knelt before her, pressing her thighs apart, licking her slit until she was open and exposed to him just the way he'd always like her.

To be devoured by Jasiri was to be worshipped. He lapped at her core like she was made of the sweetest nectar he'd ever had, and with the expert use of his mouth, tongue, and fingers, he was going to consume every last drop she possessed.

The orgasm was so quick and fierce that her body seized in one long spasm as she succumbed to its power. Jasiri gave no quarter; he kept at her until another climax was crashing down on her again, rendering her at his mercy.

He shifted, reaching under the bench, and when she could see his hand again, there was a condom between his fingers.

"I won't make any assumptions because we're technically married."

She understood what he was saying. This wasn't about sexual health. To marry a royal meant you were given a battery of tests to make sure both parties were in optimal health. At the time, she'd assumed those tests were a requirement to get a Nyeusian marriage license. After learning who Jasiri really was, she knew and understood the real reason for such thorough documentation of her health. This was Jasiri's way of acknowledging her agency and caring enough about her needs, that he would protect her for as long as she wanted.

He handed her the condom and then whispered, "Get me ready, baby."

Needing no further encouragement than the smooth sound of his deep voice, she snatched it from his hand, opening it as quickly as she could and sliding it down his length in eager anticipation of having him inside her.

This had started as a way to help him let go and somehow, he'd turned the tables on her and all she could think about was him burying himself inside her to satisfy the ache that throbbed so deeply inside, she wondered if it could ever be reached.

He pulled her up from the bench and turned her until she was facing the glass with his chest plastered against her back.

"You said you wanted me to let go, right?"

He slipped inside of her in one rough stroke, filling her to the hilt. The burn of the stretch nearly took her breath away. He slipped his hand between her folds, caressing her clit until her body began to relax in pleasure, and once it did, he snapped his hips forward, his length grazing her sensitive flesh driving her over the edge again.

He was relentless, never letting up, never letting her go until her body was no longer hers to control. It obeyed every filthy command he gave, and each time she did, he rewarded her with raw pleasure that made her weep in satisfaction as her sheath spasmed around him again as the wave of her climax pulled her beneath the current.

"God, Reigna, you still fit me so well."

His breathing was erratic, and his movements faltered as he slammed into her over and over again until she splintered apart one last time and he fell over into his own climax too.

When he turned her to face him, panting, his muscles still twitching from overexertion he looked at her with wild, lust-filled eyes before he placed his hand at the base of her throat.

"Damn, woman!"

She shook her head, trying to fight her way through the lust-induced fog of her brain to focus on him.

"You would destroy me if I'd let you."

She licked her bottom lip, holding his gaze and returning all the fire she saw in them.

"I'd do any and everything you'd ask me to."

Jasiri's chest heaved, his pupils becoming pinpoints as he stepped away from her. Despite the steam from the hot spray surrounding them, the air inside the shower was almost frigid, causing her to wrap her arms around herself as she watched the passionate man she'd just shared amazing sex with fade into this detached representative that she didn't recognize. He closed his eyes and took a breath, somehow completing his transformation. When he opened them again, Jasiri of a few moments ago was completely gone.

He reached for the shower door handle and said, "That's exactly why this should never have happened. It's exactly why it will never happen again."

CHAPTER ELEVEN

"YOU WERE QUIET tonight at dinner with my parents. Is everything okay?"

Reigna turned to the sound of Jasiri's voice, puzzled by the concern she heard there.

They were standing at the back of the palace, on the veranda to be exact, a few steps away from the garden path they'd taken to walk toward his parents' private rooms in the palace.

"Is that actually concern I hear in your voice, Jasiri?"

"Reigna, don't start."

She shook her head, then narrowed her gaze into such tiny slits she could barely see all of him in full view.

"Oh, I'm not only about to start, I'm about to finish too." She stepped closer to him. "I'm sorry, but after I sleep with a man and he instantly tells me he regrets it the moment it's over, I tend to feel a little less chatty than usual. Excuse the hell out of me."

He let a soft sigh slip past his lips and pointed to a cement bench at the foot of the veranda. Still annoyed with him, she paused as she contemplated whether to grant his request.

"Please, Reigna, just hear me out."

She nodded and sat next to him, waiting to hear what he could possibly have to say to her after last night.

"I didn't say I regretted what happened between us." She opened her mouth to refute him, but he held up his hand silencing her. "I said it shouldn't have happened."

"I fail to see the distinction."

"Reigna," he began slowly, as if he was searching for the right words to say. It was rare for Jasiri to struggle with expressing his thoughts, and seeing him do so made her settle, giving him the chance to continue.

"I don't regret what happened between us in that shower, Reigna. I just know that it has the potential to complicate things in a way I can't afford right now."

He kept his gaze forward, never once allowing himself to lock eyes with her. It was as if he needed the separation between them for some reason she couldn't fully understand yet.

"While I may still harbor resentment for the way you publicly humiliated me when you rejected my proposal, I do not wish to mislead you, Reigna. Nothing should've happened between us without me clarifying that nothing beyond the physical could ever happen between us. It's not what I want, and it's certainly not what I need right now."

When he finally looked at her, the seriousness in his gaze and the sharp angles of his face expressed how sincere he was in this moment. He truly believed what he was saying. The only proper response Reigna could come up with was to laugh right in his face.

Right there in front of him, she dissolved into giggles that she couldn't stop. Leaving him to sit there watching her in disbelief as his brows rose.

"I fail to see what's so funny about this situation, Reigna."

"Of course you wouldn't get it, Your Highness."

She intentionally addressed him with a bit of sneer in her voice, and she knew it had landed exactly as she'd intended when the muscle in his jaw ticked.

"Jasiri," she began as her laughter died down, "you have a very essential role here on this island. Please don't confuse your importance here to your importance to everything else in the world."

She stood and stepped in front of his sitting

form to make sure he understood everything she was saying.

"We had good sex. That in no way indicates that I'm looking for anything more than another orgasm from you. I don't want a do-over as far as our relationship is concerned. Or are you so stuck on yourself that it never occurred to you that after being dropped into a situation I'm wholly unprepared for that it might do me some good to let go with someone familiar for a few moments?"

She couldn't tell if it was her tone or what she'd said to him that had his pupils shrunken down into pinpoints and she didn't care. The absolute nerve of him to think good sex with him would make her lose all common sense. The fact that it had in the past wasn't the point. She was different now. They were different now, and she had no intention of letting this man anywhere near her heart again.

"Unless I tell you otherwise, please assume that its strictly physical between us. That is, if I ever decide I want someone so arrogant inside me again."

She stepped calmly away from him, making sure he understood how unbothered she was.

If you're so unbothered, why did his regret upset you so much?

She ignored the nagging voice in her head

and walked into the garden where there were tall pillars of greenery suffused with flowers of varying shades of purple with hints of gold. She was beginning to notice that purple was a theme. First his and his parents' royal rings and now the gardens. To keep up the charade that she was unaffected by this entire conversation, she decided to focus on the color scheme instead of the unexplainable disappointment his words had stirred in her.

"Is purple and gold your national color scheme or something?"

He stopped, raising a brow to let her know he knew exactly what she was doing. She didn't care. She would never admit that his not wanting her had wounded her in some way.

"Purple is considered the color of royalty. But yes, purple trimmed in majestic gold is our national color, our brand if you will. Everything from our flag to our coat of arms is fashioned in those colors. When the monarch dies, we mix it with a rich ebony to symbolize the loss."

She walked over to a pillar, fingers delicately tracing a purple petal. Its softness and its vibrant hue were calming. Unfortunately, her nerves were so loud in her head, she wasn't sure the island possessed enough purple or flowers to get her to chill the hell out.

She anticipated his heat before she heard

him step closer. No matter the physical distance, Jasiri's heat always seemed to channel to her whenever they were orbiting each other. It was both reassuring and unnerving and she wasn't sure she'd ever get used to it or if she ever wanted it to stop.

"Well played, Your Highness." His words rattled her, but she stood firm, refusing to allow him that knowledge.

"You've taken me from concern over your feelings to wanting to prove to you why our bodies coming together can never be just physical for either of us."

She kept her back to him, too afraid that whatever she saw in the depths of his eyes at this moment would be too much to handle in her unsettled state. She wanted him to prove just that. But admitting that would be the first missed step in her downfall.

She finally found the courage to turn around and look up to him. The moon framed his solid form in a celestial glow. His features were relaxed, something she couldn't quite understand considering the twisted ball of tension her body was at the moment.

Then the corner of his mouth hitched into a knowing grin, and heat quickly burned inside of her.

He closed the space between them, slowly

resting his large palm against her face, letting his thumb gently caress the skin on her cheek.

"You, Reigna Devereaux, are turning into the very queen I'd hoped you'd be when I proposed to you two years ago. Your determination to forge your own fate while caring to make a difference made me secure in my decision to ask you to be my wife. I knew that with you as its queen, Nyeusi would only prosper."

He'd never told her why he'd proposed to her. She knew it was because he loved her. Love and connection had never been an issue for them. A complicated man like Jasiri, however, would never make such an important decision based solely on how he felt about her.

Hearing him say this now, it unraveled that knot in her chest that her worry had tied.

"Why are you telling me this now, Jasiri? We're long past this. You just told me things couldn't get personal between us."

"Yes, but somehow things always manage to be personal between us even when I don't want them to be." He whispered those words to her as his fingers lowered to her neck before he burrowed them in her braids. "I thought we were past this too."

Her parted scalp tingled with the awareness of him. Her senses ignited at his touch, filling her with the remembrance of what it was like to give herself over completely to this man's ministrations.

"But seeing you throw yourself into this drama and watching you show more care for my country and its people than my uncle, who has lived here all his life, it's doing something to me, Reigna. Something I don't want, and yet it's something I can't seem to control or ignore. It's damn inconvenient if you ask me."

Her tongue swiped against the dry flesh of her bottom lip, trying hard to remember how to speak as she did.

She pressed her hands to his chest, leaning into his warmth, to his demanding presence that seemed to surround her.

"What do you intend to do about it? According to you, last night was supposed to be a one and done. I'd think touching me this way would be strictly forbidden."

His eyes flickered with amber flames of desire as he stared back at her. Without fear or hesitation, his hard gaze bore down on her, and he said, "Didn't you hear I'm about to become king? That means I can veto or reverse any previously made edicts whenever I want, without explanation."

CHAPTER TWELVE

JASIRI'S MOUTH SLAMMED down against Reigna's and immediately silenced every reasonable thought that told him he was flagrantly traipsing on dangerous ground.

Dangerous and torturous, to be precise.

He'd intended for the first press of their lips to be gentle, reassuring. But he was a fool. Things had never been gentle between him and Reigna.

His mouth on hers was like a clap of thunder in the sky, its rumble hard enough to shake their mooring, forcing them closer together for purchase.

She met him with equal fervor. Her arms wrapping around his waist in the familiar way they used to anytime their bodies found each other near. It anchored him, made him feel like he was strong enough to take on the world as long as she held him close like this.

He threaded his fingers through what seemed

like a million tiny box braids, each one pulling him back into the memory of what it felt like to have them slide across his chest, his stomach, his thighs.

Jasiri's fingers tightened as his mind gave him a quick glimpse of the moments where she'd owned his body, his mind, and his manhood hadn't suffered the least bit because Reigna touching him always meant pleasure so pure and overwhelming, all he could do was experience it.

When his fingers scraped her scalp, she moaned, her voice thick with need. He took advantage of her parted lips to lick inside her mouth, tasting the remnants of the sweet confection they'd had for dessert. She held him tighter, and his heart pounded behind the cage of his ribs.

He could feel himself thickening in his slacks, and it appeared so could she, because she tilted her hips up, touching the ridge of him, taking him from semierect to full-on hard with just one motion.

He tore his lips away from hers leaving them both gasping for air as they stared at each other. Her pupils were wide from arousal. As his own need pulsed in his aching flesh, he was certain if he looked in a mirror, his would be near blown.

"You're playing with fire, Reigna."

His voice was raspy, like sand against gravel. If he could focus on anything but Reigna and the way her heavy breasts pushed against the fabric of her button-up shirt, he'd clear his throat and use all those comportment lessons that taught him how to modulate his voice and tone depending on the situation. Being near Reigna messed with his head and therefore with his ability to exert control over himself and the situation at hand.

"Heat was always my thing, Jay. Or have you forgotten?"

His hand rested at the base of her throat as his thumb pressed against the excited pulse that thumped at the base of her neck. The mention of her nickname for him was always like a switch she flipped at her leisure to make him forget everything he'd been taught about how a proper royal should behave. It stripped Jasiri down to his elements where he was just a man, her man.

"I've forgotten nothing."

Before either of them could think about what they were doing, he had her pressed against a nearby pillar. The minute her back was against the structure and it stopped their motion, all bets, all rules, and every bit of common sense either of them possessed was gone.

Reigna's fingers were rough against the silk of his shirt, and if she kept raking at the material, he was certain she would shrcd it. She must have come to the same conclusion, because she pulled at the soft material until it was free of his waist and her hands clamored underneath until her nails reached his skin.

Talk about fire.

His skin lit up from her touch as if a torch has been placed against it, searing him with her brand. Jasiri had never wanted a tattoo, but the idea of being branded by Reigna made him ache with need.

He let his hands wander away from the safety of her neck and face. Not that they'd prevented them from crossing the line they were racing closer and closer to. He'd fooled himself into believing if his hands remained above the rest of her body, he'd protect them both from letting their passions get the better of them.

No such luck.

The need he had for her burst free of the iron cage he'd kept it behind for the last two years. As soon as the lock gave way, it rushed forward, overtaking him, leaving him unable to do anything but feel.

They moaned in unison when his palm surrounded and caressed her heavy, cloth-covered breasts.

Reigna was so sensitive there, and if they were in the confines of his bedroom where he could be sure he would be the only one to hear her moans, he'd rip her shirt open and close his lips around one taut peak and then the other.

Instead, he kept his hands moving. He was tempted to swipe the blazer she wore from her shoulders, eager to have every part of her bared to him. But they were outside, and even though he knew they were in a part of the garden that held a small blind spot from security, that blazer would provide them with some cover.

His hands reached the button of her jeans, and the realization sobered him just slightly. He was caught up in his need for Reigna. He needed to check in with her to make sure they both wanted this.

His eyes locked with hers as his fingers hesitated over the metal button. He saw heat and need there that would match his own, begging for him to give them both what they wanted. When he stilled his hands, she nodded, granting him permission to continue. Wasting no time, he flicked his fingers, separating the placket that gave him entry to what he wanted.

Jasiri had always been a thorough lover. That was doubly true with Reigna because he could never get his fill of her. This had to be quick, though. There was the threat of discovery that heightened his need to bring her to climax quickly. There was also his fear that his practical mind would finally reign in his lizard brain, and he'd have to think about what would happen beyond the moment she broke apart for him.

Before he could let his thoughts interfere with his movements, his slid his fingers beneath the lace of her panties until he met her wetness at her slit.

He groaned, his length twitching as blood rushed even faster through his veins making him ache with the need for release.

"Dammit, Reigna. I've barely touched you and you're already dripping for me."

He dipped his fingers between her folds, twisting them in a circular motion, drawing a beautiful moan from her lips. He smiled down at her, loving the glassiness in her eyes as she met his gaze.

He leaned down to her ear, stilling his hand as he spoke.

"We can't be seen here, but the cameras can pick up sound. I don't want anyone else knowing what you sound like when you're coming for me."

He let his fingertips graze her nub and she tremored.

"Be a good girl and keep quiet. I promise I'll make it so good for you if you do."

She tugged her bottom lip between her teeth and that was all the confirmation that he needed that she would comply. To add to the running list of everything that was sexy about Reigna, the fact that she was so eager to please him in bed was like a match to gasoline taking his desire from a simmering boil to an outright explosion in minutes.

She was a strong woman who knew her own mind and ran her life and her business with the confidence of someone who knew what she wanted and made no apologies about it. The fact that she trusted him enough to let go when she was with him, to let him take the reins, giving her a reprieve from carrying the world on her shoulders, made his chest swell with pride. Last night, she'd been that for Jasiri, allowing him to lose himself in her and lay down his worries for just a few precious moments. Tonight, he would be that for her, removing this burden of pretense from her. Like him, she would have to face the fact that there would never be a time where they didn't want each other. Tonight, he would ease her need to fight that realization. Perhaps, if they both admitted it, they'd find the combined strength to overcome it.

* * *

Jasiri's hand began moving again and Reigna had to shut her eyes as she damn near bit a hole in her lip trying not to make a sound. The feeling of his thick fingers sliding against her slick flesh had her hips bucking and chasing the pleasure he was giving her.

When he slipped one finger inside of her, she dropped her head to his chest, needing to be closer to him, needing the lull of the thumping of his heart to soothe her, but also needing his strength to keep her from dissolving into a liquid mess at his feet.

Soon, he'd added another finger, stretching and filling her walls just like she liked, just like she needed. His thumb circled around her nub, and she could feel herself getting closer to her peak. She tried to back away. She didn't want it to be so quick she could hardly remember it.

She no longer held any illusions. She wanted Jasiri so damn bad every inch of her ached for his touch. His previous retreat from her stoked her need to savor every stroke, every touch that this moment had to offer. If he refused to touch her again, she'd only have last night and this impromptu moment in the garden to hold on to.

Jasiri was having none of her hesitation, though.

"No retreating," he crooned in her ear. "I want it. Be my good girl and give it to me."

Why this man calling her his *good girl* twisted her up inside into a raging ball of pleasure, she did not know. She truly didn't care. All she knew was that her nerve endings sizzled with need and raced toward a delicious end every time those words graced his lips.

She bucked her hips again, and he rewarded her with another finger, three now. They rubbed furiously against that hidden spot that held the trigger to her release. A few more strokes, and she was rooting against his chest, biting down through the fabric, and not caring if she left a mark on the material or him.

It was his own fault if she did. No man had the right to be this goddamn sexy. He had no right being able to bring her to such heights with his hand and his voice. It was criminal, sinister, and she was here for every damn minute of it.

Before she could breathe her next breath, her body seized with release, and air ceased to move in and out of her lungs.

She buried her nails into his arms, grateful that they were covered with fabric that would keep her from breaking his skin there…probably.

She broke apart for him, writhing against

his body, riding his hand desperately like she would him if they were horizontal. As good as this was, she knew it would never be enough. This stolen moment in the royal gardens had reaffirmed what last night had revealed. This thing between them was living and thriving, and it refused to be shoved into the dark depths of her emotional closet where she could pretend she didn't remember it or want it anymore.

Reigna had been telling herself a bold-faced lie that she couldn't deny any longer.

As her release crested and shattered her, her sheath pulsing in rhythmic waves as her climax controlled every muscle she possessed, she decided if she couldn't ignore it, she wasn't going to allow Jasiri to ignore it either.

"There's my good girl," he whispered, prolonging her climax and his control over her.

When her release finally ebbed, he pulled his fingers from her, sliding them inside his mouth and licking them clean. Before she could get lost in how the sight of him licking her release from his flesh made her sex clench, he pressed his lips to hers, letting her taste her on him, and it was the headiest flavor of spice and sweetness, making her ache for more of him, more of them.

She slipped her hands down his sides and to his front. Not caring about her lack of finesse, she shoved her hand into his pants, needing to feel her hand wrapped around his girth.

"There's my eager girl, ready to take what she wants."

Need trembled through him as she stroked him through his clothing. She needed him to experience more so she could experience more.

Getting Jasiri off wasn't just about him reaching release. It was about knowing she could turn such a controlled, refined man into a rutting beast if she touched him the right way or swiveled her hips in the right direction. That kind of power was addictive, and after he'd laid waste to her in a matter of a few moments, she needed to return the favor in spades.

She opened his zipper; her fingertips just having made the edge of his underwear when a knock from a distance shattered the spell they were hiding in.

"Your Highness, please forgive the intrusion."

Panic welling up in her as realization took root. She was standing in a garden, at a palace no less, allowing herself to be debauched and just as eager to do some debauching of her own, where anyone could've walked in on them in the act.

She pulled back her hand as if fire had scorched it. She tried to pull away from Jasiri, forgetting there was a pillar behind her. But even if there weren't, Jasiri's strong hands on her shoulders would've kept her right where he wanted her, plastered against him.

"What is it?" Jasiri replied. His tone not hiding his annoyance.

"The guards will be making their mandatory rounds soon."

The disembodied voice said nothing else. It didn't need to. This was the royal security giving them their privacy even when the nature of their way of life provided little of it.

"Thank you" was all Jasiri said and the same loud footsteps that had drawn their attention in the first place receded.

"It seems it's time for us to leave."

He adjusted her clothing and then buttoned her jeans, then did the same for himself.

He stepped away from her, and the space between them, even though small, felt like they'd been ripped so far apart a chasm could exist between them.

With his shoulders squared, he pulled himself to his full height. When she looked into his gaze, the fire that had burned between them only moments ago was being replaced by cold reason. Whatever fantasies she had about them continuing where they left off before they were interrupted was over. Prince Jasiri, the man she was in a business partnership with, had now returned.

She straightened her own shoulders in response. Prince Jasiri may have returned, but Reigna Devereaux was here now, and she'd be damned if she was the only one who was going to deal with this thing between them that wouldn't die.

He held out his hand to her and said, "Shall we go?"

She gave him a confident smile before placing her hand in his. "We shall."

CHAPTER THIRTEEN

JASIRI ISSA NGUVU, **Prince** of the House of Adebesi, was a coward.

There was no more apt a word to describe how he, the man who was about to stand before his father's ministry council and ask their blessing of his ascension to the throne, had spent the last two weeks avoiding his wife.

Oh, he'd seen Reigna plenty, at their meals, during official briefings, during some of the lessons his mother arranged to help Reigna acclimate to her role as current princess and future queen of Nyeusi. He'd even spent time with her privately giving her tours of his homeland or simply watching movies in their apartments.

He'd mostly allowed Reigna to choose what they watched which meant they'd mostly viewed her favorite genre, Blacksploitation and Neo-Blacksploitation movies. Everything from *Foxy Brown* to *They Cloned Tyrone* kept them in each other's presence without the need to engage each other beyond commentary on the films.

It was the only way he could be in her presence without... He couldn't even bring himself to think it. To think it would have his body responding to the new memories of what Reigna tasted and felt like when she was in his arms.

His skin warmed, and he took a deep breath trying to cool himself down.

He'd thought he was rid of this hold Reigna possessed over his mind and body. The moment she'd turned his proposal down, steel walls caged his heart, and the only thing he could feel when he thought of her was anger.

Somewhere between seeing her battle a panic attack at Ace's funeral and watching her own his uncle upon first meeting, she'd burrowed underneath his skin, so much so, he'd been secretly sleeping on the oversize and, fortunately for his body, ridiculously comfortable chaise lounge.

He made sure he stayed up after Reigna fell asleep and woke up before she rose to make certain not even she knew he wasn't sleeping next to her.

It was a chickenshit way to handle his growing need for the woman who was distracting him with her mere presence. It was the only safe way to be near her and not give in to baser needs at Reigna's expense.

His insides twisted at the thought of how poorly he'd treated her in the gardens. She was here helping him. Although he'd essentially blackmailed her to be here, she'd stayed and agreed to fight for his nation.

The moments in the shower and in the gardens were pure bliss. Touching her, her touching him, her body yielding to his commands, no title could augment his sense of self-worth the way Reigna's needy moans did. He may not technically be king yet, but Reigna's body pressed against his certainly made him feel like he was.

"Son, you seem to be deep in thought this morning."

Jasiri looked up from where he sat in the corner of the large sitting room to find his father looming large in the doorway in his royal guard uniform. The jacket and pants were a deep purple, so deep they almost looked black in dim light.

His jacket was adorned with all the monarch's insignias, making an imposing yet dashing presentation. Jasiri's formal dress nearly matched his father's perfectly, except for the crown. His gold crown adorned with large purple sapphires rested perfectly on his brow as did his sword rested against his hip. As prince, Jasiri's crown and sword were smaller incarnations of his father, because no one was larger or more important than the king.

His father's eyes caught sight of Jasiri's sword resting on the marble of a nearby table-top. With their departure imminent, it should've been attached, and Jasiri should've been standing at the ready.

"Consumed with thoughts of your new bride?"

Jasiri's heart beat a bit faster at his father's question. How could he possibly—

"I was a newlywed prince once myself."

His father's broad smile and the distant twinkle in his eye indicated he had momentarily taken a jaunt back to the time when he and the queen were first married.

"When you have a good woman beside you, it can be hard to think of anything else."

His father certainly wasn't wrong about that.

"How long did it take you to get over your fascination with your new wife?"

His father's brow drew into a V and amusement showed in his eyes. "I never did, and I have no intention to. How do you think we've been happily married for more than forty years?"

"Then, how—?"

His father placed a firm yet loving hand on his shoulder. It was how he'd always calmed Jasiri when his fixation on something immobilized him. It worked then pulling him out of whatever problem had him tied in knots, and it worked now when his mind was overwrought with thoughts of the bride who remained untouched in his bed.

"Your mother's presence became my reward, my reason for doing any of this. If I completed my work, I was doing it for her and gifting myself time with her as a result. Make Reigna your reason, son, and there is nothing you can't accomplish in her name."

His father's remedy made perfect sense and at the same time erased any hope Jasiri could find a way to break Reigna's hold over him. She couldn't be his reward, his reason for a job well done. Not when he'd been so careless with her in those gardens.

"Father, I thought the reason any of us ascend to the throne is for the people, for our home."

"Who do you think is my home, son? Is it the title and power I wield? Is it the riches we enjoy? Is it the insufferable administrative things that comes with the title?"

The king shook his head in answer to his own questions.

"No," the king replied. "My home is and has always been your mother and, once you came along, you."

His father's words created an ache in Jasiri, a

longing for what his parents had. Unfortunately, entering this bargain with Reigna, he'd forfeited the possibility of that. His reunion with Reigna wasn't one of the heart; no matter how much his body ached for physical closeness to her, her heart would never be his again.

After everything he'd done to bring her here, he wasn't even worthy of any of the kindnesses she'd shown him since arriving. There was no version of this where he was actually worthy of her heart.

"A miserable king cannot justly govern his people." His father's words broke through his rumination. "If you want to succeed in your new role as king, you will have to find an anchor, a support system that will hold you up when you're weak and ground you when the arrogance your position encourages makes your head too big for your shoulders."

"Reigna is more than a prop to hold me up, Father."

"Son, you misunderstand me. Your mother isn't my prop. She's my better. Loving her means I'll do anything to be worthy of the love she so selflessly gives to me."

What an orator this man was. He was able to make anyone believe in him. That was part of what made him such a great king. Jasiri wasn't so sure he'd inherited that ability. After all, he'd chosen to blackmail Reigna into agreeing to be his bride. Sure, he'd put forth a cursory request first. Yet, he already had his plan shaped around using Ace's bequeathal as a means of bringing her to heel.

"Anyone with eyes can see that woman is your better. You just need to admit it to yourself and stop wasting time pretending you're her equal."

"Trust me." Jasiri stood, walking toward the fireplace. "I more than anyone am aware that Reigna is my better in every way that counts."

He looked up at the large painting of his mother and father on their coronation day that ran from the vaulted ceiling to just above the mantle. Its frame was fashioned from Nyeusian iron, representing the strength of their union and their commitment to the people of Nyeusi.

He scanned the painting that was older than him, relishing the regal aura captured by the artist. This was what his nation needed, reassurance that its leaders were in sync and united. Something he knew he couldn't truthfully offer them, no matter the temporary facade he and Reigna would portray for two years.

"Whatever you need to do to get your head on straight, you must, Jasiri."

Jasiri's shoulders straightened and his form tightened, falling into his royal stance with his hands clasped behind him. When Jasiri's father was speaking to him as a father, he rarely used his first name without possessive pronouns attached to it. He'd heard *my Jasiri* and *our Jasiri* so much as a child, he'd almost believed those were his proper names.

But *Jasiri* alone was tantamount to his father calling him by one of his royal titles. It was his way of easily transitioning from the personal to the regnal.

"Father," Jasiri said making sure his voice was confident and hopefully reassuring, "I will not fail you. On this day I will show the council I am the king they and this country needs."

His father's assessing gaze looked to find any signs of weakness in Jasiri's declaration. He wouldn't find any. Jasiri meant every word he'd spoken.

"Good. Then, go get my daughter, and I'll find your mother, and we'll meet back in the foyer."

"No need to go searching for us, darling." The queen's voice pulled their attention to the doorway. "The women of the House of Adebesi are here."

Jasiri spared a glance to his mother. She looked powerful in her gold pantsuit with her royal purple sash adorned with her royal and military insignias pinning the sash in place diagonally from her shoulder to her hip. Her shoulders were covered by a purple velvet mantle. The final detail that completed her ensemble was the majestic lioness crown. It was covered in large oval diamonds with an accenting row of purple sapphires.

As glorious as a picture his mother made, it was the woman standing next to her who took his breath away.

Reigna stood in a form-fitting purple suit with an asymmetrical single-breasted jacket that reached just above the swell of her curvaceous hip on one side, and on the other, a long train with billowing ruffles that swept the floor. Her purple sash adorned with royal insignias befitting the wife of the crown prince complemented the outfit nicely. But it was her diamond tiara against the intricately styled braids that turned Reigna from a beautiful woman who set his senses on fire to Her Royal Highness Princess Reigna of the House of Adebesi.

Reigna stepped inside the room. Each step stole a little of the air in his lungs. By the time she reached him, he'd suffer air-hunger for certain.

"Omari, my love. Why don't we give them a moment?"

Jasiri didn't know whether his father agreed with his mother or not because Reigna filled his vision. They must've gone, though, because Reigna gave a little wave over her shoulder before returning her gaze to him.

"I hope I look okay. All this royal gear," she said as she touched her fingers carefully to the tiara fixed atop her head. There was no need. He knew from his mother that those things were nearly fastened to the scalp with an unbelievable number of hairpins.

"You are by far the most beautiful princess to ever wear that tiara. Everyone who glimpses you will be drawn to you, unable to look away."

"Not everyone." The smile slowly dripped from her lips making him want to forget uniform protocol and take her in his arms and hold her near. "You seem to do a perfect job of keeping your distance from me."

He opened his mouth to speak, but Reigna held up her hand.

"You're sleeping on the couch, Jasiri. No matter how fancy and expensive it is, it's still a couch."

"Reigna."

"Don't lie. I know what it feels like to sleep next to you. Even though we haven't slept together in years, I remember what that felt like."

"I do too." Those words seemed so fragile slipping from his mouth. Waking up with

Reigna snuggled next to him, enveloping him with all her lovely heat. "I'm sorry, Reigna."

She shook her head, concern marring her beautiful features.

"I should be the one apologizing, Jasiri. I overstepped in the shower and the gardens. We are not together anymore, and I hadn't meant to make you so uncomfortable that you can't sleep in your own bed."

Understanding dawned and struck him in the middle of his forehead like a mallet.

"You think I'm uncomfortable with what has happened between us?"

"Obviously you are. Instead of picking up where we left off, you've been avoiding me during the day and sneaking out of our bed every night since. I'm just saying you don't have to make this weird. I won't cross that line again."

His anger simmered, trying to reach a full-on boil, and it was all directed at himself. Yet again his actions had caused this woman harm.

His pulse pounded in his ears making it impossible for his thoughts to coalesce into something concrete. He reached his hand out, startling her when it snaked around her neck and drew her to him.

Before sound could cross her lips, his mouth was on hers in a brutal kiss. He knew it was rough, demanding she yield to him, open to him. Her flesh would be swollen when he was done and that was exactly what he wanted, for her to wear his mark.

When his lungs demanded air, he tore his mouth from hers, using the hand at the back of her neck to keep her fixed right where he wanted her.

"Reigna, there is no version of me that doesn't want you. I think after all that's happened between us, it would be silly of me to deny it. I have always wanted you. Even when I was hurt and angry after you rejected me, I still wanted you."

Her brows rose in surprise as if she hadn't considered what he was saying could be a possibility.

"I tried to put distance between us after the first encounter because I didn't want to give in to that need. I've been keeping my distance since the gardens, because I felt I failed to protect you there. I have grown up under a microscope. It's the price I pay for my position in this life. But you aren't used to this. The fact that I was so consumed by my need for you that I believed hiding in a blind spot from the security camera was enough to protect you from the scrutiny being attached to me brings just shows how out of control I was. I am angry with myself, Reigna, never you."

"What if I don't want your protection?"

He watched her intently, his stare searching for any hint of deception or, worse, regret. She took her his hand in hers, and he was forced to look down to where she'd laced their fingers together in a beautiful latticework that he would never tire of seeing.

"If my eagerness in those gardens wasn't enough of an indication, I want you too, Jasiri."

"Our agreement doesn't call for this, Reigna. By indulging in what we want, it could be our undoing."

He closed his eyes, breaking free of her hold and stepping away from her.

"My undoing," he whispered as he touched their foreheads together and then placed a light kiss on hers.

"No matter how badly I want it, I can't risk it."

He took her hand, reaching into his pocket and presenting the final emblem of her position and connection to him.

It was a lioness's ring. The same as his mother but slightly smaller to symbolize her position next to the queen. He glanced to see confusion in her eyes. Confusion he'd put there, no matter how unintentionally.

He slid the ring on her right forefinger, bringing it to his mouth and kissing it before lifting his gaze to hers.

"We are Prince Jasiri and Princess Reigna until my ascension is blessed. This is the only connection we can focus on."

He could see the hurt swelling in her eyes, and his chest ached with the need to fix it, to give her what they both wanted so desperately. Then he remembered what happened the last time he'd allowed his heart to rule him where Reigna was concerned, and it fortified his decision.

Back then, he wallowed in his pain, shirking his responsibilities to the throne, to his parents, and to his countrymen. As the next in line to the throne, he'd always known to be cautious with his life because there was no spare. If something happened to him, his father's branch of the House of Adebesi would cease to exist.

The pain of being rejected by Reigna made him lose control. It made him take risks with his life by engaging in reckless activities like high-speed racing on dark streets and overindulgence of alcohol that sometimes left him unaware of how he'd gotten from one place to another.

It had taken Sherard pushing him into a shower stall fully clothed and blasting the cold water on him to clear his head enough for the man to give him the stern talking to he'd needed. From that moment on he knew he could never allow anyone to have such a hold on him again. While he believed he was past the hurt and anger those wounds had inflicted, he was left with the fear of how losing control could cause him to spiral again.

Kings couldn't spiral into despair. Not if they intended to be of any use to their kingdom.

"Did I hurt you so badly, Jasiri, that we can never get past my awful mistake?"

He searched her face for any signs of artifice. Was she playing a role, saying what she thought he wanted to hear just to get what she wanted?

No, he couldn't allow himself to go down that particular rabbit hole again. Not when there was so much at risk.

He stepped away from her, needing distance before he answered her.

"Yes."

It was a complete sentence that poured ice-cold water over both their heads. It was shocking but necessary to keep their minds and expectations clear.

Sherard materialized at the door. The royal staff had to know how to be at the ready while blending into the walls, giving the royals a sense of freedom from the scrutiny of the crown.

"Your Highnesses, pardon my interruption, but we must leave if we're to make it to the council on time."

Jasiri gave him a slight nod, and Sherard disappeared as quietly as he came.

"Shall we, Princess?"

Her face was inscrutable, and he desperately wanted to know what was going on behind those deep, soulful brown eyes that haunted him in sleeping and waking hours.

She lifted her chin and straightened her shoulders, clear signs that she was preparing for a battle. It should've alarmed him, made him lift up his own defenses.

Instead, it made need rise and his uniform pants tighten conspicuously.

"Your ascension to the throne may be a foregone conclusion, but you are not the boss of me. We are partners."

She raised her finger and jabbed it into the air with each spoken word.

"In. Every. Sense. Of. The. Word. You do not get to dictate to me. We either come to an agreement, or nothing changes until we do."

Her brown eyes flamed with specks of amber as her anger seeped into the air and into his bones, pushing aside the cold regret that rested within them. Her blaze was so damn inviting, he wanted to draw nearer to it, allow himself to be consumed by it.

"Reigna, you rejected my marriage proposal two years ago. Two weeks ago, you didn't want anything to do with me. Now, after some time in my palace and in my bed, suddenly, you can't let me go?"

He didn't mean a word of the garbage he was slinging at her, but it was his only defense at this point. She had whittled down his restraint to a bare thread, and he was ready to give her anything she asked if she said much more.

"I meant what I said, Jasiri. You don't get to dictate to me. I don't care who you are."

"How dare you speak to me like that." His voice was hard and sharp, and anyone with sense would've shrunken away from it. Not Reigna, though. Everything he knew about her said she'd choose fighting over acquiescence any day. It was why he was a fool for picking this fight. What alternative did he have when just being in her presence was wresting his control from him?

"You do realize I can turn this palace into a prison and make life a living hell for you, don't you, Reigna?"

"And you do realize I'm a goddamn Devereaux and we are bred for battle? We got hands for days and we never lose. And if you fight one of us, you're gonna have to fight all of us. Trust me, you don't want that smoke."

Did she just threaten him with physical violence? He was about to be a damn king in a matter of hours, and she was talking to him like some commoner on the street?

He was so disoriented by her words, the want he was trying to ignore, and the need thrumming through his body that he couldn't really tell. Also, he wasn't as fluent in African American Vernacular English as he should be, especially after spending two years in a relationship with a native speaker, that he could swear to the proper translation either.

The truth was, it didn't matter if she was actually threatening him or if her language was simply figurative. Either way, he was turned the hell on and two seconds from dragging her upstairs to their apartments where he'd strip every inch of that purple silk from her skin.

She folded her arms, lifting her full breasts and the tantalizing line of her décolletage to his gaze. His hands fisted, and his blunt nails bore into his flesh as he tried to keep from reaching for her. Soon, he was either going to draw his own blood or pull her into his arms. The jury was still out on which.

"Let me give you some sound Brooklyn advice, *Prince* Jasiri." The word *prince* pierced his chest like the sharpest Nyeusian blade. It was a precise blow, showing him his demise was eminent.

He couldn't win this battle, and they both knew it.

"Don't start none. Won't be none. Remember that before you try to use your I'm-about-to-be-king voice on me again."

She smoothed her hands lightly against her hair and her jacket before presenting a calm, unbothered affect.

"This thing between us," she said as she moved her finger back and forth between them, "is over when we both have gotten it out of our system. I don't need to be in love with you to screw you. So unless you're so in love with me you can't just keep it physical, we will continue as we are until we both decide this no longer serves us." She stepped close to him, wiping imaginary lint from his shoulders. "But you will not make unilateral decisions about something that involves us personally without mutual agreement."

He stood there stunned silent, unsure of what to say next. He needn't have worried how he should reply to her because she smiled up at him and said, "Now." Her voice was soft, yet firm, establishing once again that, despite his title, she was the one in control here. "Let's go make you king."

CHAPTER FOURTEEN

"ALL HAIL KING JASIRI and Queen Reigna! May the ancestors grant you wisdom, bravery, and longevity."

All the ministers repeated King Emeritus Omari's edict in unison, their words and voices so powerful Reigna might've tilted on her stilettos if Jasiri hadn't held her hand as they stepped off the dais and in front of the center aisle of the chambers.

"Rejoice, Nyeusi. Rejoice!"

The former king's voice bellowed above the crowd as Jasiri walked them through the well-wishers in the chambers. Just before they reached the exit, Reigna glanced up into the balcony seats and saw none other than Pili sitting where everyone else stood, face drawn without a hint of anything except anger.

She'd known she'd find a problem eventually in this room. There it was, looming above her like a daunting promise of her demise. Pili was officially waging war against her.

That was fine by her for two reasons.
She would not run.
She would not lose.

Death on the ocean floor over life in chains
on the land
EST August 8th, 1741

Reigna read the words carefully on the looming memorial right outside of the ministerial chambers. The granite held the likeness of five men. From their full lips, high cheekbones, and tightly coiled hair, she could tell they were of African descent. One stood at the top of a rock holding an ax in one hand and a broken shackle in the other. His features were drawn taut, and his mouth was open as if he was yelling something powerful, and the four men behind him held similar poses, expressions, and stances, as if they were making some sort of battle cry.

"What's this memorial for, Jasiri?"

"It's to commemorate the victory of emancipation that occurred when our ancestors reached these shores."

He stood closer to her, resting his hand on the cool granite and bowing his head in reverence before speaking to her.

"Have you heard of the New York Conspiracy of 1741?"

She nodded. "Yeah. When I was ten, Ace spoke about it at the reburial of the enslaved remains found in Manhattan. It was pretty much the Salem Witch Trials of Manhattan, but the enslaved and poor whites were the targets. They were accused of setting fires all over New York, including the governor's house."

The muscles of his face relaxed as if he hadn't expected her to know that. If Ace didn't teach her anything else, he made sure she knew her people's history, even the painful parts.

"The accused were either executed or exiled from New York if they were white or shipped to the Caribbean for harsher enslavement conditions. One such ship was headed for Jamaica when the ancestors changed the wind and battered the ship with a storm. Half of the ship's crew were lost at sea, and when the remaining unshackled some of the enslaved to replace the lost crew, a revolt broke out. By the time the boat was shipwrecked on these uninhabited lands, it was only the enslaved who made it to the shores. The five men are the ones who led the revolt, and once they arrived on the island, the one standing on top of the rock became our first monarch. King Dakarai Adebesi."

"You ancestor led the revolt?"

She tried to hide the wonder in her voice but couldn't. It wasn't every day you learned your husband was related to a real-life folk hero who turned the enslaved into champions and built a nation.

"I told you, Reigna. Protecting our people and our nation is written in my DNA."

He certainly had told her that. Hearing the details of how this nation came to be spotlighted that point in bold bright rays that made him look less like the asshole he'd been to her before they'd left the palace and more like a flesh-and-blood hero.

"Does this origin story have anything to do with what Pili meant when he called me part of the Lost Tribe?"

"It's connected," he replied, "but not in the way Pili intended it." Jasiri placed a gentle hand at the small of her back as he continued to stare at the statue.

"The Lost Tribe refers to Africans who were enslaved and relocated all over the world and their descendants. African Americans would be included in that grouping."

When he looked down at her she could tell he was questioning if she understood what he was trying to say. She did. Pili was trying to say she didn't belong. She looked into Jasiri's eyes and saw an apology there for the way his uncle had previously used the term. She smiled up at him, hoping to dismiss any misplaced guilt he felt in the moment.

"That's actually kind of beautiful." She saw the slight pinch in Jasiri's brows as he was trying to figure out where she was going with this. "African Americans are socially taught to be ashamed of our ancestry, as if it was somehow our fault that our ancestors were stolen, enslaved, and kept in bondage for four hundred years. *The Lost Tribe* means we belonged somewhere. It implies there's a people, a community, a land that misses us and aches for our return."

"That's how the phrase was intended to be interpreted, My Queen." Jasiri's welcoming voice made Reigna turn to face him. "What my uncle forgets is that we here on Nyeusi are members of the Lost Tribe too." He pointed back to the statue before them, pride written into every fiber of his being as he paid homage to his ancestors. "That's why we provide open citizenship to all people in the Black diaspora here in Nyeusi. We want our people to know that there is a people, a community, a land that misses their presence and aches for their return."

Her heart leaped in her chest. This man was supposed to be her business partner. Every time he spoke of his love for his country, it made her want to become a part of it and him. Sure, he'd angered her beyond reason before they'd left for the ministerial chambers. Yet when he talked about his nation and its rich history, she could forget how enraging he could be. Listening to him express his love for his nation felt like he was welcoming her into much more than the office his family held, but into his homeland and his life too.

She wanted that feeling of belonging to be real. As he tightened his arm around her, drawing her in to his side, she decided it would be as real as she needed it to be for as long as she needed it to be. After all, she was the queen. Who would dare tell her different?

Jasiri leaned down and ran his hand just under the inscription and pointed to a gold plate that read

Donated by Jordan Dylan "Ace" Devereaux, I to the loving people of Nyeusi

"Ace and his love of Black culture and history across the diaspora made him such an incredible champion of Nyeusi. When the original memorial was damaged by a hurricane, he donated a new one to us. That and his countless other philanthropic endeavors on the island made him a favorite of the people. He and my father's friendship truly benefited our people and our nation."

Her heart swelled in thinking that her great-uncle's greatness lived on in places besides Brooklyn. His good works around the world meant his legacy would live on.

She tightened slightly as a realization hit her that in all the upheaval of the last few weeks she hadn't yet considered.

"He knew you were royalty, didn't he?"

The sliver of regret in his eyes was answer enough for her. However, before she could let this knowledge turn into something ugly in her mind, he ran his hand up her shoulder before enclosing her fully in his arms.

"He loved you, Reigna. He truly did. Him keeping this secret for me was never about you. It was about protecting me. My work as an ambassador was about more than me learning diplomacy. It was also about giving me a brief moment in my life where I had some modicum of freedom to be just a man so the crown wouldn't feel like such a noose when I finally had to wear it. It was a moment to allow me to really learn who Jasiri was without all the formal trappings of the crown. Ace knew just how vital that would be to my future and to Nyeusi's future. That is the only reason he kept my secret from you."

She rested her head on his shoulder, loving Ace more in this moment than she ever could convey with words. He'd protected Jasiri and allowed him to become this man that she was falling harder and harder for each day.

Yes, she knew what she'd said to Jasiri about not needing to love him to screw him was a lie. It was all BS she'd spouted just to win in the moment. The truth was, the more she saw him love his country and embrace his place and position in it, the more she loved him. Now, she'd just have to play her cards close until she could get him to admit the same. She had no doubt he loved her. There was no way he could comfort her this way if he didn't.

She stepped out of his embrace and leaned down to run her fingers over it when she saw a shadow darken her periphery. She stood up just in time to see a young boy, probably no more than thirteen, charging at her with wild eyes.

She braced for the inevitable impact but felt Jasiri's strong arms grab her up before pushing himself in front of her. Two guards stopped the boy before he could reach the first step of the monument.

Her heart was pounding so loudly she could barely make out voices. From the way the police and their guards were talking into radios and phones, she knew there had to be chaos all around them.

Shaking her head to try to focus, she opened

her eyes, and the noise assaulted her. Instead of the radios and sirens she knew had to be blaring, she heard, "Please, ma'am, I meant no harm. I just wanted to give you this."

She looked down at the rolled-up piece of paper thrown to the bottom of the monument before he was tackled. She tried to step aside Jasiri to get it, but he shoved out an arm.

"Jasiri, he wasn't trying to hurt me. He's a baby. Just let me see what he was trying to give me."

The muscle at his jaw ticked as she placed a hand on his arm. "Please, Jasiri."

He motioned to one of the guards, and they handed the paper to him first. He unrolled it, then let out a harsh breath before giving it to her.

It was a portrait of her in front of a backdrop of Adebesi Palace. She stood tall with a crown on her head and a lion's skin over her shoulder. At the bottom it read *The Great Lioness*.

Since she wasn't wearing the same outfit in the painting as she wore now, she knew this child had made this painting for her...before today.

This time when she pressed at Jasiri's arm, he moved, letting her step in front of him walking toward where the guards still held the boy.

He was upright now but still being caged by the burly guards.

"Please let him go. I don't believe he will harm me."

They did as she asked but still bracketed the boy.

His T-shirt was smudged with grime, and she could see a small scuff on his cheek. She reached inside her purse and pulled her handkerchief out of it, slowly extending her hand to give it to the boy.

His smile quivered as he bowed as best he could with the guards standing so close.

"Thank you, Your Majesty. I meant no harm."

"I know you didn't. These two…" she pointed to the guards on either side of him "…get a little bit antsy when they see someone charging their new queen."

She opened the paper roll and showed it to him. "Why did you paint this for me?"

"Because you love our king, which means you love us. I wanted you to know we love you too."

She looked down at the painting because if she kept her eyes on that sweet boy's face she was going to burst into a bag of water. She saw a name scribbled in the corner.

"Kofe?" She chanced a glance at him. "Is that how you say your name?"

He nodded eagerly, his little chest growing ten times its size with pride.

"Thank you so much for such a kind welcome, Kofe. I will treasure this always. May I hug you?"

His shirt was yet smudged, and dirt was still on his face, but she didn't give a damn whether her designer clothing looked like an off-the-rack special after this, she was hugging this boy with such a beautiful soul who had risked so much just to honor her.

She pulled him into her bosom, holding him as hard as she could without hurting him before she pressed a kiss atop his head.

"Thank you so much for this gift, Kofe. I will treasure it and you always."

She stepped back and cupped his cheek before saying, "Next time, just be sure to get permission to talk to me first. I don't want to see you get hurt just to talk to me. You understand me?"

"Yes, ma'am."

"Good." She gave his face a soft pat before turning to Jasiri and following him and their guards back to the car.

The limousine was silent the entire ride back to the palace. Jasiri's entire being was still tightened as if the perceived threat was still in play.

The only thing keeping him anchored to the back seat was Reigna's hand clasped in his.

Touching her grounded him, kept his mind from jumping to the million and one horrible scenarios that could've unfolded if that child had meant anything other than adoration for his new queen.

Jasiri shuddered at what could've happened to that child if Reigna hadn't recognized he wasn't trying to harm her. All he had seen was someone pushing through to get to her, and his instincts had told him to protect her with his very life if need be. He'd posit that later because trying to make sense of it now would only serve to frustrate him more, and he didn't need to deal with anything else that would distort his insides the way the incident had him twisted up in knots right now.

The car had barely come to a full stop when he'd pushed the door open and stepped out of it. The staff nearly tripped over themselves trying to open the door for him, but he was too quick and too focused on the only thing that mattered: Reigna.

He was around the car and opening her door, extending his hand to help her, but to also connect with her, to remind him she was alive and so was he.

They made it back to their apartments quickly,

allowing the staff to remove their crowns and regalia and quickly take them away to the vault.

Once they were alone, Reigna removed her jacket and shoes, and by the time she plucked the last pin from her hair, Jasiri was in standing in front of her, looming.

"Jasiri, are you—?"

He didn't give her a chance to finish her sentence. His mouth was locked on hers, and he'd pulled her into his arms so quickly, she'd nearly stumbled against his chest.

If he was half the man his mother raised him to be he'd gentle this kiss, step back, and give her space, talk to her about how fear and regret had wound him up when he thought she was in danger. But that would require him to stop what he was doing, and touching her, her touching him, it was the only thing that kept him from sinking into despair.

His hands pulled her closer to him, as if he was trying to take her inside of himself. She purred for him, and it was like a volcanic explosion. His hands on her ass, Jasiri picked her up until her legs were around his hips. They made it as far as the dresser in their bedroom before their hands were all over each other again.

He leaned back just enough to grab the silk camisole covering her breasts and tear it in two, as if the delicate fabric somehow offended him.

The strapless bra holding those ripe mounds of flesh would've been next if she hadn't held out her hand.

"This is a La Perla exclusive. You can't buy this anymore, and I will not let you destroy it no matter how much your growly caveman bullshit is turning me on."

He tilted his head, feeling the corner of his mouth hitching up into a grin. She wasn't joking in the least little bit, and it was both amusing and intoxicating all at the same time.

"I want it off. Now."

She slipped from the dresser to remove the bra, and he stepped away to get what they needed in the nearby night table. When he looked up again, Reigna was standing beside him, her body free of clothing as she slowly crawled into the bed, her back arched like the fierce lioness he knew she was.

She lay down on her back planting one foot on the plush bedding before she slipped her fingers between her folds, stroking herself slowly and deliberately. The delicate skin of her sex glistened with her arousal, and if he hadn't been rock-hard already, the sight of her pleasuring herself would've taken him from soft to ready to cut diamonds within seconds.

"Are you waiting for an invitation?"

He disrobed quickly, holding himself over

her as she continued to bring herself closer and closer to release.

"If you come before I have the chance to fill you, I promise you'll regret it."

She pulled her bottom lip between her teeth, as a glint of mischief sparked in her gaze. "I guess you'd better hurry up, then, because I'm nearly there."

He sheathed himself, taking both her hands in one meaty palm and locking them in place above her head as he used his hips to make her open to him. He ran the covered tip of his domed cap over her sensitized flesh, his entire body loving the sweet ache that flared inside him. She was so wet, her arousal coating him, making the glide that much smoother, taking him from painfully hard to steel and making his balls heavy with his release.

Her moans were becoming louder with each swivel of his hips as he caressed her swollen flesh. She was almost on the edge, and he wouldn't miss the unadulterated joy of having her hot and dripping, nearly squeezing the life out of him as she bore down on him throughout her release.

He slipped quickly inside, riding her hard, nearly drowning in the pleasure of her body molded around his as if she were made explicitly for him. The first spasm of her release made him snap his hips harder, angling himself from muscle memory over that spot that made her explode. Just like he remembered, her body convulsed beneath him as she called his name over and over as if it was a lifeline to her salvation.

He'd needed this. To see her alive, vibrant, and beautiful, taking his strokes so good he had to fight not spill from the second he'd entered her. He placed his hand at the base of her throat, letting his thumb rest softly against her racing pulse, confirming that she was here, with him, and in danger of nothing except the pleasure pouring over her.

When her release subsided and her eyes focused on him again, she saw something. She gripped the hand around her throat, relocating it to rest flat against her left breast, and she kept it there as he plowed into her.

"I'm here, Jasiri. I'm okay."

The knowledge that she understood what was driving him, this uncontrollable need he had to bond with her, to reassure himself that his worst fear hadn't happened today, it melted something in him. He couldn't afford to be vulnerable in front of Reigna, not when he knew the pain of her turning his world upside down. But in this moment, he couldn't hold back his need to be not just near her but in her and around her.

He fell forward, catching himself on his

elbow as he buried his face in her neck. Here, she couldn't see how afraid he'd been for her and himself. Here, she couldn't see the relief her safety brought him. Most of all, here, she couldn't see how much she'd wrapped herself around his damn heart. Reigna could never know she had that kind of power over him.

She wrapped her arms around him, rubbing his back and whispering soothing things in her ear until his body was one big knot of tension that snapped so tightly that when his climax rushed through him, he'd nearly blacked out from the unending pleasure. Her body spasmed around him, milking him, drawing his orgasm out longer until his skin was so sensitized he shook.

He'd told her this should never happen between them again the last time he'd found himself buried in her body. As his muscles slowly relaxed and his breathing became somewhat normal, he realized how wrong he was. He needed her. He needed them. He couldn't go on pretending otherwise.

CHAPTER FIFTEEN

"DID YOU MEAN IT?"

Reigna stretched, a smile tickling the corners of her lips when she felt the hard planes of Jasiri's naked body pressed against hers.

His arm hung possessively over her hip, pulling her into the cradle of his lap until he was so close she could feel the strong beat of his heart.

"Sir, you just sexed me stupid. I'm gonna need more information if you expect me to hold a coherent conversation with you."

The rumble of his laughter in his chest made her snuggle closer to him, his warmth so inviting she doubted she could pull herself away even if she wanted to.

"When you said you didn't need to be emotionally attached to me to have sex with me."

The languid relaxation that had her bones malleable just a second ago began to stiffen. As if he'd sensed her need to flee, he pressed a gentle kiss on her bare shoulder and gave her a squeeze around her waist.

"I need to know, Reigna."

She turned in his arms and met his gaze. There was a vulnerability there she'd never witnessed before. This man was a whole king. People had literally fallen at his feet and heaped praises on him as a matter of course like someone serving her coffee in her favorite brunching place. But here he was, needing reassurance from a wound she realized had been festering for the last two years.

"No," she replied with a smile. "That was just bravado. I had to save face after you basically told me you didn't want anything to do with me."

He held up a finger. "That's not exactly what I said."

She shrugged. "Doesn't matter. That's what I heard, what it felt like." She leveled her gaze at him before speaking again. "What about you, Jasiri? Is this just physical for you?"

He huffed in feigned frustration. "My life would be so much easier if it was."

She slipped her thigh over his as she placed a small kiss on his chest, and his body instantly reacted, his skin pebbling up at the site of her touch.

"That's not an answer, Mr. King."

"I think you mean *Your Majesty*."

She raked her fingers down his chest pulling a needy moan from him.

"That's not an answer to my question, Jasiri. Is this just physical? Is that how you'd like us to proceed?"

She raised her eyes to his, needing to see his response as well as hear it. She couldn't be in this alone. Not after everything they'd been through.

"No matter how I've fought it, you are part of me. I don't want to fight this thing between us anymore, Reigna. I want us to be real again."

Her heartbeat was just this side of too fast as she listened to him. He didn't just want her, he wanted them. She'd known that. But hearing him say it, it soothed the unease she'd been carrying since she'd recognized she was losing her heart to him again.

"It's just…we said this arrangement was temporary. It would be unfair of me to try to change the rules now."

"I seem to remember a certain king-to-be telling me he could change his mind at any time without explanation. Is that still true, Your Majesty?"

She moved her body against his, making him shudder. His responsiveness to her touch had always heightened her physical need for him. Now that he'd admitted she wasn't the only one losing in their misguided battle of wills, she needed him to dive into this headfirst just like she was.

"Is that still true, Your Majesty?" she repeated.

"Only if you agree to forget about our contract and stay."

A tiny sliver of panic inched up her spine as her inner commitment-phobe tried to raise a red flag. She closed her eyes, refusing to permit it to surface. Fate was giving her a second chance, and she wasn't going to let her irrational fear keep her from getting everything she wanted.

Hell, she was already married to the man. That had to count toward getting over her commitment issues, right?

She locked gazes with him, making sure he saw nothing but her sincerity in her eyes. "As far as I'm concerned, that contract has been chewed up in the shredder. I'm here for as long as you want me, Jasiri."

She laced her fingers through his and gave them an encouraging squeeze. She let her hand slide down his chest until her fingers were tracing over the hard ridge of his abs. She kept going, her fingers threading through the thicket of curls at his groin.

Her fingers descended until they met his half-hard length. She cupped him, and he spread his legs wider, giving her an open invitation to continue her exploration.

A growl simmered at the back of his throat, making the sensitive flesh between her legs tingle.

She gave him a single stroke, and his flesh lengthened. It was thick, long, and heavy in her hand, its weight making her mouth water.

She didn't wait for him, buried her nose in the cleft where his thigh met his groin, taking an intoxicating sniff of his spicy scent. She stroked him once more, and then licked him from his base to his tip, before swirling her tongue around his proud dome.

His hips bucked, searching for the warmth of her mouth, and she didn't disappoint him. She glanced up while she took him as deep as she could, loving the heft of having him on her tongue. And when her eyes met his and she could see him fight for control, she knew she'd won this battle…for now.

Jasiri didn't trust her completely, that was evident in the way he couldn't let go. But she wouldn't relent. She would show him better than she could tell him what she wanted and that he could trust her with his heart again. Until then, she would break down his walls one lick, one kiss, one caress at a time.

* * *

"This is heaven."

After three weeks of him and Reigna working themselves to the bone to make the transition of power as smooth as possible, Jasiri had decided a weekend away with his new bride on the royal private islet was just what the two of them needed. The brilliant sun, gleaming white sand, and doing nothing but lounging, eating, talking, and making love would cure the weariness their new roles caused.

Jasiri watched as Reigna plopped down on a thick beach towel spread out upon the plush chaise of the cabana. Her deep brown skin glistened with rivulets of water that cascaded down every inch of her. Between the sheen of water on her dewy skin and her pinup-girl-style two-piece swimsuit, Jasiri's body responded the same way it always did when he was this close to her: with want.

"I take it you're enjoying Bandari Ya Kisiwa." She cracked one eye open as she regarded him.

"Bandari, who now?"

He found so much amusement in her forthrightness. Unlike many he'd met from such a privileged background as hers, there was no pretense where Reigna was concerned. She wasn't brash. She didn't speak carelessly or without thought. Her business would never have become as successful as it had if she hadn't learned how to prevent people from knowing exactly what she was thinking.

But there was no cowering behind artifice for her. She spoke plainly so that her audience knew she'd meant exactly what she'd said.

"Bandari Ya Kisiwa. It translates roughly to Haven Isle in Swahili."

She pulled herself up on her elbows, giving him her full attention and a full view of her plump bosom, and for a moment he was more than a little distracted. When he heard her calling his name, he returned his gaze to her face.

"Jasiri, you speak Swahili?"

"Among several other languages. You kind of have to be a polyglot if you're going to be a dignitary. Swahili, Yoruba, and English are our national languages, so I was taught all three from birth."

She tilted her head, and he could see the questions forming in her head. Since she'd arrived, anytime she'd wanted to know more about his country's or his people's history, she always reproduced this gesture.

"I thought Swahili was an Eastern African language. If most people stolen during the Transatlantic Slave Trade were from the west coast of Africa, how did Swahili become one of your people's national languages?"

"The people who founded this nation were a mix of enslaved people who'd been born in the American colonies, recent Yoruban abductees from Nigeria, and new abductees who were taken from what is now known as the Democratic Republic of the Congo where Swahili is still spoken. That's how all three languages became our national languages."

Something bright shone on her face, and he wasn't exactly sure what it was. It was sort of wistful yet reverent, and he wanted to know more about it.

"African American culture is rich and deep. Its connection to the ancestral lands we came from are still strongly visible. But our culture isn't treated as if it's part of the American cultural identity. It's a subculture, something niche, and often positioned as oppositional to American culture. Sitting here listening to you talk about your historical legacy and knowing it's celebrated by your people and your government, it's…inspiring."

He'd heard it said that the way to a man's heart was through his stomach. For Jasiri, his national and ancestral pride was a gateway to his.

Her awe of his history, his people, his land, it was like a magic rope threading itself around his heart, and Reigna knew how to tug on it just so it was near bursting in his chest.

He pulled her into his arms, something he was doing more and more since that night three weeks ago where fear for her safety had driven him to forget about the detachment he tried to encourage between them. Sitting here with her now, he was so glad his foolish plan hadn't worked because being near her, with her, did something to his soul that he couldn't willingly relinquish if he tried.

"Every time I hear you speak about Nyeusi, its history, and its people, the more I know my wisest decision as king was choosing you for its queen."

She wrapped her arms around his waist, tugging herself closer to him and covering his leg with hers. He tightened his hold on her, a pleasurable sigh escaping his lips as his soul reveled in the peace being in her arms brought.

They remained silent until a loud grumble rent the calming sounds of the water's movement back and forth across the shore.

They chuckled in unison, Reigna taking her hand and placing it across the soft expanse of her belly.

"I guess I worked up an appetite swimming."

"If my queen wishes to feast, then she shall feast."

He grabbed his phone from the nearby table and sent off a quick text.

In a matter of moments, several staff members stepped into the grand cabana made of sandstone and cedar, placing platters of food on a long table.

Once the staff was gone, Jasiri took her hand and guided her to the table where she could choose her fill.

She pointed to a white pastry box sitting in the center.

"Are those from…?"

As a surprise, he'd had an order of pastries hand-delivered from Buttercooky Bakery, her favorite bakery in Floral Park, New York. It was an extravagant thing to do that he normally wouldn't indulge in. Seeing her full lips pull into an excited wide grin, he decided he'd have fresh pastries from this place every day and twice on Sunday if she gifted him with such a beautiful smile.

"Yes," he replied. "I know you love their raspberry-filled croissants, so I had two dozen flown to the island."

"You really are like a prince from the fairy tales."

He shook his head while grabbing a plate and utensils and then presented her with the golden-brown croissant with thick red ribbons of stripes of raspberry swirling around it.

"No, I'm a real-life king, milady. Way better than those fairy tales."

He handed her the plate and she sniffed, the aroma making her smile grow wider.

"These smell delicious." She took another sniff before looking up at Jasiri.

"Is everything okay?" He waited for her to respond. He'd wanted this surprise to be perfect for her; if something wasn't right, he needed to know.

"Nothing's wrong," she said and sniffed it again. "Just different. I think they may have started using some kind of almond extract or flavoring because there's this almond scent mixing in with raspberry and butter that I don't recall."

Panic rose up in Jasiri, forcing him to smack the plate out of her hand as he yelled, "Don't eat that!"

He pulled her away from the table as he pressed the screen on his smart watch, activating a blaring alarm that made them both cover their ears.

His adjutant and several guards poured from the beach house and crowded around the cabana in a protective, military stance.

"What's happening, My King?" Jasiri could

hardly make out Sherard's words over the loud beating of his heart blending into the shrieking alarm.

"Someone just tried to poison the queen."

CHAPTER SIXTEEN

Reigna was done.

She was so done as soon as she opened the door to their apartments and found four guards positioned at the door and in the corridor. She was sure there were more she couldn't see making themselves blend into the walls to go unnoticed.

She slammed the door and screamed out her frustration, only to have one of the guards stick his head in the door to make certain she was okay.

"I'm fine!" she barked, never feeling more violated than knowing she was living under a microscope since the attempt on her life. The guard gave her a remorseful look, trying to impart how bad he felt for her. No matter how bad he felt, she knew he'd never let her out of his sight on pain of death.

She'd been in Nyeusi for eight weeks. The last three of which she'd spent locked inside the palace like some fairy-tale princess in a tower, and it was driving her mad.

They'd discovered the kitchen staff had been infiltrated by a Pili supporter. He'd claimed to have no official connection to Jasiri's uncle, but no one believed that. Unfortunately, they couldn't find proof to substantiate their beliefs. This deluded young man would stand trial for attempted regicide, and Pili would be as free to come and go as the waves rushing and then pulling away from the shore.

Reigna sat down on a high-backed chair by the balcony, lifting the receiver and punching in a number she knew better than her own.

"If it isn't Queen Reigna I of Nyesui blessing her lowly sister with a phone call."

Reigna forgot how annoying her sister could be, even from a distance.

"Don't start, Regina."

Her words were terser than she'd planned, and she could feel Regina's energy change through the line as soon as she said, "What's wrong, Reigna?"

She paused a minute. Ringing the alarm in the Devereaux family was like having all the emergency responders from everywhere converging in one place.

"I'm just missing my sister, and it's making me grumpier than usual."

"You sure Jasiri hasn't done something?" Her sister's voice had a healthy dose of suspicion that couldn't be denied. "You know I don't play about my sister. If I have to come remind His Highness of that, I will."

Instantly, Reigna's mood lightened not because her sister was essentially offering to wage war for her, but because she knew her sister well enough that she'd have Jasiri crying for his mother if Reigna really believed he'd done something to make Reigna unhappy.

"Technically, it's *His Majesty*, and Jasiri is fine," she said, fudging that truth. He was physically okay, but he was a walking ball of rage that couldn't be reasoned with right now. A fact Reigna would not share with her sister.

"He's just busy with running the government. I get to help a great deal, but then there are times when even the queen can't take part in the secret meetings."

That bit had added to her frustration at present. Before the attempt on her life, Jasiri had always allowed her to take part in his governance of the country. Now it was as if he'd shut her out of everything to keep her wrapped up in a tiny closet, if that closet was a sprawling palace.

She knew this was just because Jasiri was scared. His concern aside, he was honestly ticking her off.

"I just miss you." Reigna tried her best to keep her frustration out of her voice. She and Jasiri hadn't really discussed this yet. In that moment, as much as she was annoyed with him, she still wanted to protect him too. "Why don't you come visit? I know you're coming in another month for the coronation and wedding. I just would love to have you with me now, if you can get away."

That wasn't a lie in and of itself. She did miss her sister. They had been inseparable for most of their lives. But there was another reason for this visit Reigna didn't quite want to acknowledge. Jasiri's insistence on isolating her was triggering all those old fears imprinted on her by her parents' toxic marriage. She recognized there was a part of her that was ready to run when things got hard. She hoped having her sister here might soothe her jumpy nerves that were making her itchy for escape.

"If it means that much to you," Regina began, "I can come out in a few days."

Regina coming to visit her meant everything to Reigna. It meant she wouldn't feel so isolated and alone while Jasiri was on his master-of-the-land rampage. It meant she might just live up to her vows and stick around through better and worse.

"I have that gala you asked me to attend in

your place," Regina continued. "I still don't get why I must pretend to be you at this thing."

"Because I can't get away. If I go, there's just going to be too much to plan security wise for Jasiri and me to be there. Has word of our marriage or accession reached the States yet?"

"Surprisingly, no," Regina replied. "I honestly was expecting it to be all over the world by now. Your husband must have some major PR sway."

Reigna chuckled at that. She was certain Jasiri did have sway with the media to keep their union and his ascension out of the global news.

"You know the British royals are the only royals the world cares about. Luckily that means you can attend this gala in my place and get those folks with deep pockets to sponsor the Alva Grace Trust."

Ace had started it after his wife, Alva, passed away. It granted scholarships for young women entrepreneurs in Brooklyn.

Rich people were stingy with their money. They liked to feel catered to when they were giving it away. That meant if the chairman of the fund didn't show up to schmooze with them, they'd be less likely to dig as deep as Reigna needed them to in order to keep the fund growing.

"Fine," Regina groaned as she acquiesced.

"I'll go to this stupid thing and smile like you for an hour and then I'm out. You better have one of the crown jewels prepped as my reward."

"I'll do you one better," Reigna replied. "I'll let you into my closet where they've stocked it with the most gorgeous, and ridiculously expensive clothing you've ever seen. Do this right, and I'll let you take something. If you exceed our fundraising expectations, I'll even let you into the purse and shoe closets too."

Knowing how her sister loved shoes and purses, Reigna was pretty certain Regina had been shocked speechless on the other end of the phone.

"Fine." Regina's harrumph made Reigna's shoulders shake with amusement. "I'll be there. But you'd better make sure you have your butt back here for the private memorial we're having at Devereaux Inc. in Ace's honor. I'm not going to be answering fifty-'leven-hundred questions about where you at and why you didn't let nobody know you got married."

Reigna laughed at her sister's use of the mythical and exaggerated number used in Black culture to express when something had been done, said, or asked with exhaustive frequency. She wasn't sure which one of her ancestors came up with that particular idiom. But it would live in infamy in the minds and vocabulary of Black people now until forever.

"God, our family is nosy," Reigna lamented having momentarily forgotten about that fact. There was too much going on when she'd agreed to Jasiri's business proposal to even think about all the questions her cousins and the like would have.

"Exactly," Regina agreed. "You will not leave me here to deal with that alone, Your Majesty."

"You know, Regina, that phrase is usually said with the utmost respect for me."

"Heifer, please," her sister laughed obnoxiously in her ear. "I shared an amniotic sac with you. The chances of me ever caring about your fragile feelings are nil."

"I hate you," Reigna replied.

"You adore me. That's why your ass is begging me to come stay with you in your palace."

"When you're right, you're right."

Reigna wouldn't even try to deny it. She did adore her sister, and if admitting that would get Regina here sooner so Reigna could deal with the current level of angst Jasiri had her living under, she'd say it a thousand times more.

"Sire."

The sound of Sherard's voice forced Jasiri to look up from his computer. He glanced at the time and saw it was nearing midnight, making this the earliest night he'd stopped working in the last three weeks.

"What is it, Sherard? I'm about to retire."

He ran an exhausted hand down his face, pinching the bridge of his nose briefly to relieve some of the pressure this never-ending stress headache was causing.

"I tried to bring this to your attention earlier this evening, but you said you didn't want to be disturbed when in discussion with General Askari."

Jasiri straightened. Whatever Sherard was about to say, he instantly knew he wouldn't like it. He also knew he'd have no one to blame for his anger but himself because Sherard was reminding him of his own edicts.

"What is it, Sherard?"

"The queen called her sister today. She made arrangements for Ms. Devereaux to visit in a few days. Neither disclosed how long the visit would be."

Jasiri stood and walked to the floor-to-ceiling window that looked out over the gardens. It was a place that was supposed to offer calm, peace. He felt none of those things at the moment.

"Sire, did you wish me to prepare the palace for her twin's arrival?"

Jasiri's stomach dropped as if an unforgiving brick was lodged in it. Reigna was already unhappy with him. Their cold bed and their even colder exchanges since the incident were all the proof he needed his wife was definitely not pleased with his security mandates. Making the wrong choice could be the breaking point for them and the union they were building.

He knew Regina would give her life for Reigna. He also knew how devastated Reigna would be if Pili harmed her sister in an attempt to get to her. He didn't need another person to have the royal guard focusing on. All his efforts had to be centered on protecting Reigna, even if she ended up hating him for it.

"Contact Ms. Devereaux first thing in the morning and cancel her trip. Between plans for the coronation and the wedding, providing Pili with more targets would not be wise."

"Should I tell the queen?"

Jasiri looked out into the dark night, unable to help but see the blackness as a forewarning for what was to come.

The attack on Reigna had made one thing clear for Jasiri. The thought of living without her caused him unbearable pain that seeped down deep through his bones, into his cells, and right into his soul.

He loved her.

Not just as a companion who was helping him run his country, either. He was in love with her.

The paralyzing fear he felt when he realized her pastry might be laced with cyanide was his first clue. The moment that suspicion had been confirmed and he recognized how close he'd come to losing her forever, desperation took root in him, coloring every thought he had.

"No," Jasiri answered. "I will tell her in the morning. Please make the cancellation your priority at the start of the day."

Sherard left just as quietly as he'd come, leaving Jasiri to wrestle with his demons. He had no doubt he was going to incur Reigna's wrath over this. In comparison to what placating her anger might cost him, he couldn't be concerned with it.

Her anger he could handle. Her not being in the world would effectively end him.

Jasiri slid into bed, reaching for Reigna's warmth the moment his weight was completely pressed against the mattress. He'd been working around the clock for the last three weeks and his time with her had been limited to the few hours he slept next to her.

He wrapped his body around hers, needing to know she was safe in his arms where she belonged.

She stirred in her sleep, her full bottom pressing against the swell of him.

"Jasiri?" His name was a sleepy whisper on her lips, and it was his undoing.

He'd planned to pull her into his arms the way he did every night, to make sure she was safe, warm, and protected. Hearing her call his name like that, as if it meant everything to her, soothed him, made him feel whole.

If the anger and fear his uncle had wrought had torn away half his soul, Reigna's anger had gutted him hollow.

Not with harsh words or a loud voice: no, she'd chosen an even deadlier weapon. Her silence.

She'd refused to talk to him beyond what was necessary or be with him during the day. The result was him barking at everyone around him like he was some sort of tyrant. Holding her was the only way he found a moment's peace.

He'd taken to sneaking in their bed, needing to gather her to him, just to quiet the fear and anger that seemed to be his constant companions.

"I need you."

He felt her stiffen, and he worried that she'd leave him there to suffer just like he deserved for putting her in danger and for not finding a way to stop Pili yet.

"Just let me hold you."

She turned in his arms without a word, pressing one hand gently against his pec and slipping the other around his waist.

He'd wanted to hold her to make sure she was safe, but as her body intertwined with his, he realized it was him that felt safe and protected.

She pressed her hand against his shoulder and kept pushing until he was flat on his back, and she was straddled atop him.

"I wasn't trying to—"

"That's your whole problem Jasiri. You're focused on the wrong thing. Instead of stalking around this palace yelling at everyone," she pulled the silk nightgown from her body exposing all of her to him, "you could be here with me focused on all of this."

She leaned forward, letting his cloth-covered sex settle between her naked folds, and he gripped her hips forcing her to sit still.

Her lips quirked into a lopsided grin. The little minx was enjoying torturing him. She ground down on him forcing a needy groan from him that was strong enough to shake the walls.

"I'm either going to come like this," she said as she swiveled her hips again while she cupped her heavy breasts and tweaked her erect nipples, "or you're going to take off those silk pajama bottoms you love so damn much and give me what we both want."

She lifted and he removed them. As soon as they were gone, she lowered herself to him, and when her wet heat engulfed him, pleasure seeped through his skin, firing every nerve he possessed.

Her naked heat sliding down his flesh drained his lungs of air and made them burn with the need to breathe. Her movements were slow and deliberate, almost surgical in how they elicited pleasure from him. If she kept this up, she'd kill him, and he'd have the shortest reign in history.

Jasiri decided right there that if she was going to kill him, if he was going to be undone by their joining, he'd be damn sure to take her with him too.

He wrapped his arm around her waist, pulling her down to the bed and flipping them, notching himself between her thick thighs. He slid inside of her in one stroke, filling her to the hilt.

Her back bowed, and he used the canting of her hips to deepen his stroke. Her body clamped down on him, and he nearly collapsed. He dropped forward, locking his elbow above her shoulder, hooking her thigh over his arm so he could plunge in and out of her.

He found that tempting spot where shoulder

met neck, biting down on it gently to heighten her pleasure.

She moaned, her hands grasping his ass, pulling him deeper as her core quivered around him, as she neared her peak.

His gaze locked onto her face. Reigna in the throes of passion was a beautiful sight. Her face contorted with need as she climbed higher, trying to grasp the prize that Jasiri kept just out of reach for her.

It was only when she said "Please, Jasiri" that he slid his hand between them, circling her swollen nub as he stroked so deeply inside her, he thought they'd become one.

His balls were heavy and aching, and he could feel the electric spark of his release tightened at the base of his spine. When she broke apart, strangling him with her sheath tightening around him like a damn vice, Jasiri's climax pushed through him breaking the hold his anger had on him and filling the empty space Reigna's absence had left him with.

When he spilled the last drop of himself inside of her, he slumped against her, taking her mouth into a deep kiss. The kiss was meant to connect, but it was meant to conceal too. It kept him from having to speak or to give her the chance to look at him and see how raw he was inside.

Reigna had ruined him, and he'd let her. And as they cleaned up and she burrowed into his chest falling into a satisfied sleep, he realized he'd let her ruin him again, as many times as she wanted to. Just as he was about to slide into a blissful sleep realization hit him and he stiffened.

"Reigna, we didn't use a condom."

"I know," she replied on a yawn. "I was there."

"Reigna—"

She held her hand up, stopping whatever he was going to say next.

"We got carried away, Jasiri. Neither of us planned it. I'm okay with any consequences that may arise from it. Are you?"

Their pre-marital health screening established their was no medical reason for their continued use of condoms. But they'd never discussed starting a family.

Suddenly the image of Reigna swollen with his child filled him with warmth and pride, burning itself into his soul.

"Reigna, are you saying you're okay with a possible resulting pregnancy?"

"Yes I am."

Her words rang clear in his head and he couldn't help the smile curving his lips. He went to tighten his embrace around her, but she pointed a finger at him instead.

"I'm mad as hell at the way you've been keeping me locked away in this palace, Jasiri. That said, I'm still not going anywhere. Not for anything or any reason. I'm here for the duration. I'm with you for as long as you want me."

Fear gripped him. There was no question he wanted Reigna through this life and the next. Nonetheless he knew once she found out what he'd done, there was a possibility he'd pushed her beyond her breaking point, and he would lose her, and now possibly his child, for good.

CHAPTER SEVENTEEN

"Everyone out. Now."

Jasiri's office was filled with his administrative staff, all of whom worked for him and honored him as their king. Not one of them looked to Jasiri, who sat in the middle of the room behind his massive desk, for confirmation. They all stopped what they were doing and began making their way out of the room.

Maybe it was Reigna's stiff stance or maybe it was the steel in her voice. Whatever it was, she must've had *I am not to be played with* tattooed on her forehead because those folks scattered like they were running from explosive hot lava raining down on their heads.

When the door clicked closed behind her, she stepped toward him with her finger pointed at him.

"You sneaky—"

He raised his hands palm side up, cutting her off as if she were one of his servants. She'd thought she'd been mad after the call she just received from her sister. With just that simple gesture he'd taken her from angry to enraged, decimating any chance they had at having a reasonable conversation.

"Reigna, I—"

"I don't want to hear it, Jasiri. Canceling my sister's visit without consulting me? You've gone too far."

She stood looming over him, her fury vibrating through her resulting in seismic quakes through her body.

"You've kept me locked up in this damn palace for three weeks as if I'm the one who did something wrong. I hate it, but I knew you were doing it because you were scared, because the thought of losing me scared you stupid."

His widened eyes almost made her laugh. Apparently, he'd really thought he was hiding that well.

"If you know that, you should understand why I canceled your sister's visit."

"Jasiri, I am your wife. We agreed that I would also be your partner in this royal endeavor. Instead, you've sidelined me as if I'm some helpless, fragile damsel who can't fight for herself."

"Reigna, I—"

"I said shut it!" she bellowed, not caring if

anyone on the other side of that door could hear. "You are the king of this nation, Jasiri. But you are not God. You do not get to make decisions for me without consulting me or getting my permission."

Fire flashed in his brown eyes, and she saw the moment his restraint snapped. He stood so quickly his chair crashed to the carpeted floor with a loud thump. Jasiri ignored it, focusing only on her as he stalked around the desk and stood before her.

"Pili tried to kill you, Reigna! He tried to kill you, and I can't find a goddamn thing to tie him to his attempt, which means he's free to try again."

His locs hung free, swinging and moving with the same angry staccato that his words took on.

"I will not let him take you from me."

He spoke through clenched teeth. His features were twisted with fear and rage. She'd seen Jasiri undone when they'd made love. But she'd never seen him so out of control with anger that she could hardly recognize the man in front of her.

"If I have to lock you in the goddamn dungeon and throw away the key, I'll do it with not a single ounce of guilt because as pissed as you may be with me, you'll still be alive."

He shoved his fingers through his hair, tugging them angrily through the neatly twisted strands. It looked painful, but in that moment, she thought he might somehow welcome the pain.

"Don't you understand, Reigna? I love you."

He slapped his hand against his chest as he spoke each word again.

"I. Love. You. And the idea of letting him take you away from me sets fire to my soul. If he takes you, what will be left of me? If he takes you, then everything I have sacrificed to protect my nation, my people, my family, it will all be for naught. Because if he takes you, there will be nothing left of me that will be fit to live, let alone rule."

Heat burned through to her skin as tears pooled in her eyes. This beautiful and strong man had been so broken by his fear he was closing the rest of the world out to keep the thing, the person he was fixated on, with him.

"Oh, Jasiri. Don't you see? If Pili had really meant to kill me, I would be dead. What he wanted was to get in your head and he's done that. This is not love, Jasiri. This is obsession, and I cannot condone it. I won't live like this, not after watching how my parents spent years manipulating each other for their own gain. I won't let you turn us into them, Jasiri. That would be the thing that actually kills me."

He leveled his gaze at her, shaking his head as he stood before her. "You're not taking this seriously, Reigna. I'm trying to do what's best for you."

She placed her hand against her chest to still the tremors shaking her digits. "That's what my father told my mother when he insisted they get married once he and his family discovered she was pregnant. It's also what he said to her when he demanded she give up her dreams of earning a college degree because he was a Devereaux and his wife didn't need to work when he was more than capable of providing for her. It's also what he told her when he isolated her from all her friends and family who were trying to warn her that my father's controlling behavior wasn't healthy. I won't let you do that to us or me, Jasiri. No matter how good your intentions are."

"We are under threat, Reigna—"

"My sister is not a threat, and you know that. But your fear is controlling you, poisoning your way of thinking and making you see threats where there are none. They're making you try to strip me of my freedom just to keep me by your side."

She stepped closer to him, placing careful

hands on his face and pressing her lips gently against his.

"I love you, Jasiri. I never stopped loving you. But I cannot watch you destroy yourself by playing into Pili's long game. I won't live as a prisoner, and I won't watch you turn our love to bitter hate because you can't let go."

She stepped away from him. Closing her eyes until she could find the strength to meet his gaze.

"I'm going back to Brooklyn today."

"Reigna, we had a deal."

His words were soaked in anger, but she knew that was a disguise for the hurt she could see gathering in his eyes, in the way his shoulders slipped just a little.

"I will honor that deal. I will show up for any royal appearances you need me to. I'll return for the wedding and the coronation. But I cannot live here with you, like this. When you are ready to hear reason and see that I am an asset to you, a weapon to be wielded instead of a source of weakness, then I will return to this island so fast it will make your head spin. Until then, I can't stay here with you and watch you turn us into my parents."

She walked toward the door and stopped abruptly when he said, "You know I can stop you if I choose. All it would take is a word."

Her tears began to flow, there was too much pain gripping her heart for her to hold them back now.

"I know you can. But you should also know that I spoke to my sister on my private cell phone, the one I came here with. If she doesn't receive a call from me with my flight information in the next fifteen minutes, she'll use every resource the Devereauxs have to start a media shitstorm."

She placed her hand on the doorknob before her as she continued. "You told me once that the most vulnerable time in any government is during the transition of power. Do you really want to test whether the monarchy can weather the global media scrutiny of you keeping an American citizen here against her will?"

When she didn't hear him stomping after her or calling for his guards, she released a breath. Before she could twist the knob and open the door, she heard a sad small whisper rent the air.

"Before you go…" His voice was shaky and frail, and if she hadn't known that they were the only two people in this room she wouldn't have recognized it. "Please tell me what's so terrible about me that your first response to trouble is always to leave me."

His words hit her like stone against brittle bones, making her want to drop down into the fetal position to try to protect herself from the emotional blow.

She turned around, and her knees nearly buckled when she saw the shimmer of unshed tears filling his eyes. "I said *no* not because I didn't want to be your wife but because I didn't know how to be anyone's wife."

He flinched, as if her words struck him across his jaw like a skilled fist trained in the art of hand-to-hand combat.

"We hadn't talked about marriage. I had no idea you were even thinking along those lines. I needed time to prepare, Jasiri. Time to understand that I wasn't my mother and you weren't my father. Instead, you sprung a very public and unexpected proposal on someone you knew from jump was commitment-phobic and when the expected happened, you walked away from me without a word."

She glanced up at the ceiling briefly to gather strength to continue.

"You left. You cut me off, blocked my number with no means of contacting you. And when I went to the consulate to try to speak with you, I was told I was no longer allowed on the premises. You decided we were over, Jasiri, and I wasn't given a say in it. I will not let you do the same thing to us again out of some misguided attempt to protect partly me, but mostly to protect yourself."

His jaw tightened, and she could tell he hadn't ever considered how their breakup had affected her. She'd been too afraid to say these words then, a mistake she wouldn't repeat now.

"I won't cut you off the way you did me. I will always keep the lines of communication open between us because what we have is worth fighting for. But right now, you're not ready to fight. You're running scared, Jasiri, and that fear is pushing me away."

She wiped her fingers across her face to stanch the river of tears sliding down her cheeks, hoping to say this one last thing before she completely devolved into sheer emotion and no reason.

"The first time I left you was because I was afraid of me, Jasiri. Now I'm leaving you because I'm afraid for you."

And with that, she turned around and opened the door, stepping into the empty hall, walking away from the man she loved quite possibly forever.

CHAPTER EIGHTEEN

REIGNA SAT AT her desk, making the final arrangements for the rechristening of the library in the Devereaux Inc. building. Her cousins and sister had handled most of it, but there was a new development that only the queen of Nyeusi could carry out.

"Do you think Jasiri is going to handle this well?"

Reigna looked up at her sister's question and saw Regina and their five cousins filing into her office.

Regina, Jeremiah, Trey, Lyric, Amara, and Stephan all stood in the middle of the room like a protective barrier from the wind, waiting to cover her when her world was crumbling around her.

"If he knew what my plan was," Reigna began, "I don't think he'd be handling it well at all."

Reigna had known the moment Jasiri had

crossed that final line that if she was going to save their marriage, she'd have to find a way to deal with Pili and end the head games he was playing with her husband. To make that happen, though, she needed her family, and she needed to change the arena in order to capitalize on home-court advantage.

Jeremiah spoke up. "Everything is settled on my end, Reigna. My connect has everything set up. They'll be by the morning of the event to get everything arranged and go over the detailed plan with you. We're gonna finish this once and for all."

His wife Trey placed her arms around his waist and smiled at Reigna. "Jeremiah's right. We're gonna teach this fool that if you come for one Devereaux, you come for us all."

They all nodded in agreement, including Reigna. This family didn't play about theirs, and Prince Pili of Nyeusi was about to find that out the hard way.

Her family exited her office, and she knew it was time to set the most important part of her plan in place. She took in a breath and dialed, expecting to get a notice that her number was blocked. Instead, Jasiri picked up on the first ring.

"Reigna?" His voice was rushed, tinged with a bit of relief. When she didn't answer immediately, he spoke again. "Please tell me you're safe. Are my guards near?"

"I am safe, and your guards are just outside my office door. I have complied with all their demands. I wouldn't risk my life unnecessarily. Not when I want to come home, Jasiri. I don't want to be without you any longer than I have to."

"Then, don't, baby. Come back to me."

The sound of his voice melted through the cold numbness she'd carried around in the two weeks she'd been gone.

"I want to. But I need to know you trust me to make decisions for myself. I need to know you trust me to fight at your side. I need to know you trust me to fight for you when you can't or won't fight for yourself."

"Reigna, what you're asking—"

"Jasiri, I know part of this is my fault because I ran without an explanation, and I hurt you as a result. I'm trying to tell you now that this is different. I'm not running because I'm scared, I'm fighting for us and for Nyeusi. The question is, will you trust me enough to fight with me?"

Reigna made her way through the crowd, stopping to chat with friends and colleagues of Ace as they praised the work she and her cousins had done to create such a touching memorial to her uncle. It was then that Reigna caught sight of Jeremiah, and he gave her a quick nod letting her know it was go time.

"Sweet Lord in heaven, please let this work. Not only is the future of a whole nation on the line, but so is my heart."

Her prayer said, she gathered the flowing skirt of her evening gown heading toward the executive elevator. With her royal guards falling in step behind her, she found herself and them emerging from the elevator and onto the executive floor in no time.

She stepped inside of the dark room, forgoing the wall light for the dim lamp she used when she was working late or needing to think in silence and semidarkness.

She sat behind her desk, looking out into the window that made up the back wall. From here she could see the serenity of the lights of the Brooklyn Bridge stilling her nerves. That bridge was Brooklyn's strength and resilience personified, and if she needed any more encouragement, she could hear the rap goddess Lil' Kim telling her Brooklyn didn't run from ish to soothe any uncertainty she had about executing her plan.

The glint of metal reflecting in the window glass shut down any remaining doubts she had. She was Queen Reigna I of Nyeusi as well as

Reigna Devereaux of the Brooklyn Devereauxs. Just in case there was any misunderstanding, she was ready to set shit off.

"Prince Pili," her lip curled a knowing grin as she slowly spun around in her chair to face her husband's uncle. "Right on time as scheduled."

"As scheduled?" he huffed with a dismissive tone, as if he was shooing her away with a condescending *silly girl*. "There's no way you knew I'd be here tonight."

Reigna raised her brow, keeping the rest of her body still in the chair.

Pili walked toward her slowly, taking the seat in front of her desk as if she'd invited him to sit down. Entitlement just oozed from this man, and Reigna couldn't wait to be done with him.

"What can I do for you, Pili?"

"Oh, My Queen, I am the one who is here to do something for you."

She leaned back into her chair, crossing her leg and granting him permission to speak with a wave of her hand.

"It's been brought to my attention that the king isn't doing well since that unfortunate attempt on your life."

Reigna shook her head, already over this man's feigned concern. "An attempt we both know you're behind, so why don't we stop with the pretense and get directly to the point of your visit, shall we?"

He chuckled as if she were amusing him, and she smiled in return. This man was underestimating her, and he had no idea what a foolish move that was.

"Well, then, if that's how you want it, I'll be perfectly honest. Yes, I was responsible for the so-called attempt on your life. But since I abhor murder, you should know that I had no intention of bringing harm to you. I just knew that thinking you were in danger would send my besotted nephew into a tailspin."

She steepled her hands together as she looked at him. "I don't understand how you thought provoking Jasiri this way would benefit your cause."

"You wouldn't," he sneered. "You haven't been at court long enough to know that a king more concerned with his wife than his kingdom isn't fit to rule. By whipping Jasiri up into a frantic tizzy, I have all the proof I need that the king is not fit for the crown. I didn't need to kill you to accomplish that. I simply needed to make it look like I was."

She breathed slowly through her nares to control the anger swelling in her chest. She was almost there; she couldn't let him win now.

"The only problem is you had someone plant

real cyanide in my pastries. If I'd taken a bite of one, I'd certainly have died."

He smiled as if any of this was the slightest bit funny, shrugging nonchalantly as if this were all some sick, twisted game.

"But you didn't, so it all worked out in the end, right?"

She closed her eyes, smiling before she looked at him again.

"Pili, you are absolutely right. It did work out in the end."

"I'm glad you see things my way," Pili responded. "Now, if you want me to stop my mental warfare on the king, have him abdicate, or I promise you I will ruin him before the eyes of the Nyeusian people."

Reigna leaned forward, chuckling as she did so. "You really do think you've got me right where you want me, huh?" When he opened his mouth to speak, she held up a hand to stop him. "It was a rhetorical question. This attack on Jasiri was cute, and it might have actually worked if he were married to any other woman but me."

Pili's smile slowly dripped off his face as he watched her, as if he finally realized he might not be as in control of things as he thought.

"Pili, while you were playing checkers, I was playing chess. You see, in Brooklyn, you've always got to know somebody, because knowing somebody is how we get things done. So when I called my cousin Jeremiah to tell him about my plan to get you out of my hair once and for all, he was all too happy to call one of his friends from way back in the day who just happened to be an NYPD captain. Captain Heart Searlington, would you like to introduce yourself to Prince Pili?"

From the shadows of the office, a tall Black woman with her dark hair pulled into a tight bun stepped into the dim light. She wore a bulletproof vest emblazoned with *NYPD* as she slowly stepped toward Pili's chair.

"Prince Pili, is it?" Her question was rhetorical, but to a megalomaniac like Pili, failing to acknowledge him was a cutting blow. "It seems you've been a bit chatty. You actually admitted to attempted murder in a room where anyone could be listening." She pulled a radio from her waist and spoke into it. "Did we get that, boys?"

"Copy that, Captain," crackled through the airwaves leaving Pili gripping his armrests as his jaw dropped in shock.

"You were recording me?"

Pili had found his tongue, apparently, and his backbone too, because his shock turned visible as he sat ramrod straight in his seat.

"Well, you villainous types like to hear yourselves talk a lot, so I figured it shouldn't be that difficult to get you to admit your crimes on tape."

His brown skin flushed with anger, as his eyes turned nearly black with rage. If it weren't for the fact that a police officer was in the room with them, she had no doubt Pili would've chosen violence in that moment.

Catching himself, he recovered quickly and fell into his royal facade easily.

"It doesn't matter what you've recorded. I have diplomatic immunity. I could've assassinated the king in front of this officer, and there wouldn't be a thing she could do to me."

"That's easily fixed." Reigna smiled as she spoke to him. "I'm revoking your diplomatic immunity right now."

Pili laughed loud enough to shake the walls. "You've been queen for all of, what, five minutes? I think you need to take some more civics lessons to figure out how diplomatic status works in Nyeusi. Only the monarch can grant or remove diplomatic status." His lips pulled into a loathsome grin. "Being the whore he beds doesn't give you any power over my status."

"Oh, Uncle."

At the sound of that deep and powerful voice,

Pili's confidence slid off his face, turning his skin from a deep brown to an ashy death gray.

Jasiri stepped into the room flanked by his adjutant Sherard on one side and General Askari on the other.

"When my wife…" Jasiri let the word dangle in the air as an open objection to his uncle's attempt to disrespect and degrade Reigna "… arrived in the United States, she did so as my regent. As my regent, she wields the full power of my office in the capacity I have granted her. Today, that would be in state matters where she can decide which of our emissaries will be covered by the might of our nation."

Jasiri pulled a folded piece of paper from his pocket, opening it and holding it in front of Pili's gaze. "Two hours ago, she signed the paperwork revoking your diplomatic immunity. An hour before that, she had my written permission to do so."

Pili's eyes widened, and his jaw dropped open as realization hit.

Jasiri moved to stand near Reigna's chair, pulling her to her feet and placing a protective hand at her waist as he pulled her into his side.

"You can either return to Nyeusi and be tried and convicted of treason and attempted regicide, where the penalty is death." Jasiri gave a brief nod to Captain Searlington before he continued. "Or the captain can arrest you and you can face trial in the American justice system for your admission of the attempted murder of a foreign dignitary. Either way, you will never be free to come near my wife again."

"Nephew." Tiny beads of sweat bubbled on Pili's top lip and forehead. "You can't do this. We are blood. Think of your father." Pili had been reduced to bargaining for his life. He was a dead man walking, and he knew it.

Jasiri pointed at himself before speaking. "I am king of Nyeusi. I decide how to handle all threats against the crown. My father mourned his brother the moment you made an attempt on the queen's life. He knew then there would be no version of this where you would walk free of your crimes. Make your choice, and make it quickly. My general is aching to throw you in the dingiest cell he can find."

Captain Searlington handed a thwarted Pili over to her lieutenant. When she returned her gaze to them, Jasiri reached out and shook her hand.

"Captain Searlington, you have the appreciation of all Nyeusi for protecting our queen. Should there be anything I can do to repay the favor, you have but to ask."

"I appreciate your offer," she said, sharing a reassuring glance with Reigna before she returned her gaze to Jasiri. "My husband has had a twisted family member put him in harm's way too. I know the worry you must've felt. This was a freebie. You don't owe me anything."

She turned to walk out the door but looked over her shoulder and said, "There's a bunch of Devereauxs that are clamoring to get upstairs. You want me to let them up?"

"No," Reigna responded, "I need to speak with my husband alone."

Captain Searlington left the room followed by Sherard and General Askari.

As soon as the door clicked, Jasiri had Reigna in is arms and his mouth pressed against hers. He devoured her. Not just in a sexual way, he was drinking from her, drawing life from her into himself.

He finally tore his mouth from hers, leaving them both fighting to drag air into their lungs.

"You took years off my life," he choked out. "Don't ever do that again, Reigna."

She smoothed her hands out over his cheek, so grateful to be in his arms again.

"You trusted me to fix this, Jasiri."

The sentence came out half statement, half question. Like she'd witnessed a miracle unfold before her own eyes.

"I had no choice, Reigna. I needed you back. This was so different than our breakup two years ago. Then, all I had were crafted fantasies about what it would be like to have you by my side as queen. Now," he said and cupped her face, sliding his thumb along the gentle line of her jaw, "now I know what that feels like, what the reality is, and my fantasies can't compare. I was so out of line, Reigna."

He closed his eyes, shaking his head while he admonished himself. "I would definitely understand if you wanted nothing to do with me."

He took her hand and bent his knee as he looked up at her with contrition glimmering in his gaze.

"Kings don't kneel before anyone but God, Reigna. But this king would take the knee as many times as you deemed fit if it meant you'd give him another chance to prove he will be better."

She tugged at his arm, bidding him to stand before her.

"This queen does not seek to put her king on his knees. All she has ever wanted was to stand by him, to fight with him, and to fight for him. When you are weak, it's my job to fortify you. As long as you remember that, I'm packed and ready to go home right now."

The smile on Jasiri's face warmed her heart airing out the dank places that pain and mistrust had left to rot.

"If you won't accept my supplication, I hope this will express how much you mean to me and how committed I am to having you by my side."

He reached into his inside jacket pocket and pulled out folded documents. He gave them to her, and she wasted no time scanning through them.

"You've turned complete ownership of Ace's house over to me?" The words tumbled from her mouth quickly as she continued to read. Then her gaze slid across the last line of the transference, and a tear slid down her cheek and onto the page, blotting the corner it had fallen on. "This says you signed these on our wedding day?"

He let a gentle finger slide across her cheek to collect her tears as he smiled down at her. "When I told you who I was, I expected you to end our deal and demand I take you home. You completely surprised me when instead you demanded to be my partner, to stand by me and share the load. I knew then that you deserved better than me holding something significant to you over your head. I had my lawyers draw up the papers that very day. I signed them digitally and had the forms notarized and filed in America. This house was always supposed to be yours. I was simply correcting my great wrong."

His palm cupped her cheek, and she burrowed into it, letting his warmth fill her. This man had loved her and protected her even when they both refused to acknowledge their love in that moment.

"Take me home, Jasiri."

He nodded and then clapped his hands, and the door to her office opened with Sherard standing at the ready.

"Sherard," Jasiri said without taking his eyes of Reigna, "the queen and I are ready to return home. Make it so."

"By your command, My King."

EPILOGUE

"WHAT DOES MY queen yearn for if her mind is so far away from me?"

Jasiri's arms closed around her, bringing a smile to her face as she leaned back, resting her head against his chest. They stood in the palace gardens at their favorite column that hid them from the rest of the world.

"I was just thinking that when we met again, I was going through the worst pain of my life. Ace was gone, and then I found out he'd given away the one thing he'd promised me."

He didn't speak. Jasiri knew her well enough that he understood she didn't need to be rescued, just heard and considered. Of all the things she loved about her husband, it was that he'd taken the time to learn who she was now.

"Ace's house."

He hugged her to him, and again she let his strength seep into her.

"It was never about the house. It was about holding on to the only person who'd loved and protected me the way I'd needed. I was so damn angry with that old man for doing me dirty and giving you half that house. I realize now, he'd known exactly what he was doing. He knew I would fight like hell to get what I thought was mine."

Jasiri chuckled. "Ace was always ten steps ahead of all of us. If I didn't know any better, I'd say he planned our reconciliation down to the royal wedding."

"Knowing my great-uncle, I wouldn't put it past him."

She turned in his arms, placing a gentle peck on his lips. "Because of Ace's meddling, the worst pain in my life turned into my greatest joy, Jasiri."

She was so grateful to Ace for all his wisdom, grateful for all she'd gained because of it, but most of all, she was grateful for the love she shared with Jasiri.

The celebration in the palace blared, drawing their attention. She hooked a thumb over her shoulder toward the palace. "We should probably get back to the party before they send the King's Guard looking for us."

"It's the second reception today." Jasiri tightened his arms around her. "They can do without us for a little while."

"True, but this reception is the private one

for our family and friends. I actually want to attend this one."

He stepped away from her, bowing dramatically. "Whatever my queen wants, I shall provide."

He gave her his elbow, and they walked until they were positioned in front of the doors to the grand hall.

The doors opened, and music surrounded them as they danced their way to the center of the floor to the sensual tune of Gyptian's "Hold Yuh."

She'd spent all day following the proper protocols for the royal wedding, immediately followed by the coronation, and then the reception for all the heads of state. But this one, this was what she and her fellow Brooklynites would call a full-on bashment party.

Yeah, it was on the bougie side because it was being held in a palace. The important things like a fire DJ and all their family surrounding them, cheering for them as they lost themselves in the rhythm and lyrics were still present, though.

This moment was the real start of their lives together. The one she would remember every moment of her life. And when the song blended into another, and her husband smiled down at her, she knew this was the perfect time to give him his wedding gift.

His hand was lovingly resting low on her waist. She threaded her fingers through his and slid his hand forward, flattening his protectively over the bottom of her stomach.

Jasiri caught the motion immediately, his gaze locking with hers as his eyes asked the silent question.

A smile and a tiny nod was all it took before he grabbed her up in his arms and swung her around.

She placed her mouth near his ear so he could hear her over the music. "Put me down, you maniac, before my morning sickness starts again. Your heir doesn't like sudden motions."

He placed her gently on her feet before pulling her to him and kissing her breathless right there on the dance floor. The music was blasting, and the lights were flashing, but the only thing Reigna could see was the man she loved so overwhelmed with joy at the news of her pregnancy that her heart was fit to burst.

"I love you, Jasiri."

A happy tear slid down his face as he placed a finger under her chin and lifted.

"And I love you more, My Queen. Just as it should always be."

* * * * *